T0354770

THE CLOUD

THE CLOUD

THE CLOUD

JACK A. HANCOCK

THE CLOUD

iUniverse books may be ordered through booksellers or by contacting:

iUniverse
1663 Liberty Drive
Bloomington, IN 47403
www.iuniverse.com
1-800-Authors (1-800-288-4677)

ISBN: 978-1-5320-0975-4 (sc)
ISBN: 978-1-5320-0976-1 (e)

Library of Congress Control Number: 2016918067

Print information available on the last page.

iUniverse rev. date: 12/28/2016

CONTENTS

CONTENTS

PREFACE TO THE CLOUD

A LITTLE WHILE AGO OR MAYBE more, I was visiting my sister, Betty Kerans. She was a member of a writing club in Dayton, Ohio, and she read one of my stories to the club. It was a tear jerker about a dog, and everybody had a tear. After the meeting, she ask me to write a story about some color which the club had requested that she write. I said,

"Ok, would yellow be acceptable? She said that it was. I started the story when I got home, but then started to wonder why she had not done it herself. I have since realized that she was having memory problems which was reducing her ability to organize her thoughts. So, I finished the story, "Old Yellaar". She turned it down because it was too long, several pages more than the club expected. Some -time later I re-read the story and realized that it was the beginning of a science fiction novel. It was all my sister's fault, and I thank her for getting me started. I think one of the reasons was my ability to tell good stories when I was just a boy. One time I told a Halloween story so well that a young girl screamed at the climax. So you see maybe that is the reason I enjoy writing stories in later life.

I give some credit to Worlds in Collison by Immanuel Belkovsky, The Great Warming by Brian Fagan and The Technology by David Hatcher Childress.

The story is about the mysterious disappearance of the color yellow. Why yellow disappeared; what effect it had; who was responsible, and how it was returned. It has all the elements of a good story, a war, romances, danger, adventure, worldwide catastrophe and Aliens. The main characters are Colonel Aaron Post, a physicist and his wife Janice, a former French astronaut...

There is some mathematics and physics involved and in places a little stretch of imagination. For those of you who enjoy Science Fiction, read on and thank Betty for the inspiration.

CHAPTER 1

THE CLOUD

Jack A. Hancock

SURPRISE

T IS JUNE 12, 2110 the night before the happening, Colonel Aaron Post and his wife, Janice, had moved to the patio to enjoy the pleasant June evening. She said, "I wish you didn't make those secret trips. I worry."

"You shouldn't worry because they are mostly giving advice He didn't add that it could also be dangerous. Besides, I enjoyed them for the sense of power. Isn't that sky beautiful and clear? No rain tomorrow. You know it is late; maybe we should get ready and go to bed. I have a busy day tomorrow at the Albert Einstein University teaching physics. They go to bed.

He woke up a few minutes before the alarm sounded and lay there contemplating his day. As he looked around, he did not recognize the room. Something was not quite right. Then he realized that the green walls had turned blue. That is not possible; I must be having a nightmare.

He pinched his arm and let out yelp, and his wife woke up. She said,

"What is wrong with you?"

"Oh nothing, I was just laying here thinking about my day, and the walls changed color."

"What nonsense are you giving me now? Must you always be thinking and coming up with something new. You can be very confusing at times."

"This is serious; wakeup and look at the walls. The color has changed from green to blue."

"That is imp-------. Good grief you are right. Maybe, it is the light, and it will look ok after we shower and get dressed. Then we can raise the blinds so the sunlight shines in."

"Do you think both of us are having the same nightmare?"

"No, let us get dressed, and things will look normal. I think that I shall wear that yellow dress and go shopping since you are not going to be here. Come on let's take a shower together, and you can rub my back."

"Ok, that is an invitation I can't refuse." After the shower, she goes in to the closet and immediately starts screaming,

"My yellow dress, My yellow dress!"

"What is wrong?"

"It has turned white. And the closet looks like a morgue. Is this your idea of a joke?"

"Honey, I haven't done anything, and I don't think this is a joke. Why don't you wear the blue dress; it looks good on you and go shopping. Do you know where that triangular piece of clear glass is?"

"Yes, it is in the center desk draw in that place you call an office."

"Thanks, while you are dressing, I will see if I can find out why the yellow is missing."

"You better put on some clothes, or the neighbors will call the police. What are going to do outside? I thought you were going to work."

"Maybe, but first I am going to look at the sun's spectrum. I will explain when I get back." *By this time, I was beginning think some serious event had occurred last night which might just lead to War, but I kept my suspicions to myself. No use starting something without the facts. Now, you know the color yellow can't disappear or can it? The prism revealed that the color yellow was missing from the spectrum at least in our neighborhood.* He goes back in to the house and yells to his wife.

"THE SUN'S SPECTRUM IS MISSING YELLOW; it is much colder, and the sun seems dimmer."

"Are you nuts?; you know that is impossible. You are frightening me. Why?"

"I am also a little frightened because something major has happened. I will try to explain later. Maybe we should try to determine how much area is void of the yellow color. It could be just a local problem."

"I know a great many people across the country and in Washington whom I could call."

"I guess you really don't know what I do, but you may have guessed based on my secretive and quick departures.

If this is a worldwide disaster, I will get a call from the President on my private government phone and will be ordered to get to Washington by the fastest means. In the meantime, call some of your friends and get their impressions." Although the Colonel is in the Airforce he is attached to the President's staff for special assignments. *He is familiar with atom bombs, rockets, power systems and espionage.*

"Ok"

"When you get off the phone, we can compare notes and see how big this yellow thing is."

"Oh, you physicists always have to have more data before you can make a statement or decision. I don' know how we ever got married; you were gone so much of the time?"

"You did not have to worry, I loved you from the first time I saw you In the President's office when you were the Attorney General. I was not going to let you get away."

"PS, I was never worried; I knew you loved me and I you."

While waiting for Janice to complete the calls, he sat contemplating the loss of yellow, the dimmer sun and the drop in the outside temperature. She came back into the room.

"Honey, what did you find out?"

"My girlfriends are in shock. I think a couple of them passed out on the phone, and the others were a little incoherent. It seems they also did not find yellow."

"Well, I guess that means only our little town is missing yellow."

"Oh no, I called them in New York, California, my father in France and that funny Japanese man, you know in Hawaii. They all give the same answer."

"That makes it appear that this is a worldwide phenomenon. I am surprised that Washington has not called. By the way, how did you know where the prism was? You know how fussy I am about you moving my stuff. Oh, there goes the phone. I think I had better take you with me, and we can talk on the way. Pack a small bag, something you can carry on the plane. We will be traveling light and won't have time to wait for baggage. Take a winter fur coat; I think it is going to get quite cool or maybe cold."

"Why would you think it is going to get cold in June; it was 80 yesterday?" He answers the phone.

"This is Colonel Aaron Post."

"This is this John Belltone, the President of United States. I need your pass word."

"The pass word is Continuity34."

"Thank you, we need you in Washington as soon as possible. The team is already here. We will fill you in on what happened last night when you get here. Air Force One will be in Denver about noon today, and a car will arrive to pick you up in two hours or less."

"Is it ok to bring my wife?"

"Yes, it will be nice to see her again. There are no accommodations in Washington, so you will be staying at the White House. Things will be casual for this event. Have a good trip. Goodbye." *Aaron hangs up and dashes around packing up clothes, the portable computer and the prism. He knows that whatever else is needed will be supplied.*

"Honey, you can pack a larger bag because we will be riding in Air Force One." *The limousine arrives, and after loading up, Aaron begins to tell his wife what he thinks had happened, and what the effects were.* He says,

"I don't know the reason why the yellow has disappeared, but I am certain that some external-terrestrial event has occurred. Either the sun has changed, or something was filtering out the yellow color. If the sun has changed, we ought to see a marked drop in the Earth's temperature, maybe a 100 or more degrees F within a few hours. If that happens, life as we know it will be short lived. We would need to do something very quickly to prevent the people from freezing to death. According to the experts on the sun, it is supposed to maintain its prolific energy output for another 5 billion years or so before it goes berserk. A change in the sun is very unlikely. As a matter of fact, the change in temperatures is only 40 degrees or more in just a few hours. We are not seeing more, so I opt for a filter until I know more. We maybe at war with someone."

"You mean a filter big enough to cover the world; that is crazy. Why are we going to Washington, when you could just tell them what you think on the phone?"

"I won't be the only one going there. The President will be gathering all the experts to discuss and give advice on the best solution if there is one. Perhaps, we should explore the effect of no yellow color on our life and the world."

"Aaron, have you realized how fast and dangerous the driver is going. He is darting in and out of traffic and barely missing cars. I am hardly listening to you. Why didn't they provide an escort?"

"Well, I guess we are going to get one. I hear a siren behind us. The driver should have the right information to convert the cop to escorting". *The limousine stops briefly, and they continued to the airport at an even faster pace with the cop leading the way, and the siren screaming full blast. Janice says,*

"Somewhere I heard that the color one sees is the one not absorbed by whatever we are observing."

Yes, I have heard the same thing but I am not sure that is completely true. That theory says if you see a red rose, it is because the rest of the spectrum is absorbed by the rose and for objects of other colors other portions of the spectrum are absorbed. But what happens if yellow is not around? It is hard to give a definitive answer. I can only make a few guesses based on the primary colors, red, yellow and blue. Black is the color that absorbs all the spectrum and white reflects the spectrum. The color yellow is a part of every one's life. Just think for a few seconds how it would be if there was not the color yellow in the world."

"Oh! My yellow dress!"

"Sun light has all of the colors, but one can't see them until the light is viewed after it passes thru a prism with non-parallel sides. When I looked at the sun light after it passed through the prism, yellow was missing, but the other colors were present. Many think that light moves at a constant velocity and for most purposes this is true in a vacuum. The colors in white light move at different speeds and different wave lengths. As a result when white light is passed through the prism, it is separated into the glories colors of the rainbow with the gold at the end."

"You know better. I have been flying many times, and a few times, I have seen a rainbow in a complete circle. The gold at the end is a fraud, and you know it. You are just kidding me."

"Yes, you know the rainbow is light refracted by the drops of water suspended in the air. The colors from top to bottom as we see it on the earth are: Red, Orange, Yellow, Green, Blue and Purple. If seen from an airplane, the red is on the outside of the circle with the colors in the same order as you see them from the ground. What happens when the Yellow is removed from Sun light? It is anybody's guess. A guess is that if you eliminated yellow, the other colors would also disappear. But I know we are still getting the other colors which means the sun is still producing, and therefore the loss of temperature and yellow are caused by a filter."

"If you really mean that, and it is not crazy, who would do it and why, and how?"

"I can't answer your questions; I just know it has to be. Since it is the temperature which develops white light and the heat, I think if the Sun changed, it would get whole lot cooler, and the colors would change. I don't think we would need to worry about global warming. The earth would probably turn in to a big ball of ice if the Sun were cooler. That would be a major catastrophe for life on earth. As I have said before, I don't think the Sun's temperature has changed. I think the yellow is filtered out preferentially. The filter would need to be huge as you mention before. With yellow removed, the world will be changed in many ways.

The morning temperatures indicate that energy received has been reduced. This means the earth is getting colder. If the filter were permanent phenomena, the earth would be somewhat cooler which means the weather would change. There will be more snow in the winter and cooler summers. Before we can say how much cooler, we would need to know how much sun radiation we had lost. We would also find our daily life sorely affected with yellow unavailable. But, if the temperatures get much colder, there will be more serious problems than color. Survival would outweigh all other issues."

"What a happy jolly fellow you are; the world is coming to an end. I hope your forecast is wrong."

"Sometimes scientist don't realize what effect their statements can cause. I hope I am wrong. Think what it means to have colors in our life. Yellow is the cheerful color, and I think probably closer to the human physic." Janice says,

"Without yellow I am feeling less happy and maybe more bellicose. I am already feeling sad. Cheer me up."

"Why do you think I am taking you to Washington? There will be work, but we will have time for dancing and having wonderful meals."

"That is wonderful; I thought it was all work. Go on, I love listening to you."

After luxurious ride in Air Force One, we arrived at Andrews Air Force Base.

"Why can't we travel like this all of the time?"

"It only happens to our class if someone in power deigns to bring you into their presence."

"Why can't you be in power; I like it?"

"Although I like a little power, I am not designed that way. Too much power would cramp my style. Enjoy it while you can. I see the helicopter which will transfer us to the White House. Let's get off and don't worry about your bags. That marine will bring them." *They enter the White House and are greeted by the President's assistant who introduces Aaron's wife to the house keeper and says for Aaron to follow him. Even though it is close to supper time, the president wants to see him immediately. The President shook his hand and said,*

"I guess you know about the color and temperature changes. But first let me tell you about the explosion. You probably know, that NASA has been following a very large body for several months. It was expected to miss the earth by fifty million miles, but there was a sudden change in direction about 2 days ago. The new trajectory would only miss the earth by about 200,000 miles which puts it close to the moon's orbit, 238,000 miles.

Last night at about 2 AM it exploded and scattered pieces in a path between the earth and the sun. We know that the pieces of rock and particles are continuing on the new path but are spreading along the path and perpendicular to the path. The rock was moving at about 100,000 miles per hour, and the exploded pieces are still moving at 90,000. What light can you shed on the absence of yellow and the lower temperature?"

"Well, I have examined the suns spectrum, and I believe that the color yellow has been filtered out, and the spread of dust between us and the sun seems to verify that statement. That is why we have the new coloring system. I think, as the dust spreads and thins out, the amount of radiation will increase, but I don't think the yellow will come back very soon. I think that the original spectrum will return when the filter disappears, and the colors will return to normal. If NASA can tell us how fast The Cloud is moving and spreading; maybe we can estimate how long this will last. We also need to know how much the Suns radiation has decreased. NASA or whoever is keeping track needs to determine how the radiation is changing with time. The amount of sun radiation determines the average earth temperature. If it appears that the temperature will drop substantially, the people must be prepared."

"Let us go to dinner, and while we are eating, my assistant, Jeff banks, can contact NASA. Supposing The Cloud moves on, but the yellow does not come back."

"I don't want to think about that happening for now. It is bad, but if it is a permanent thing, we will probably have a bigger problem. The sun could be going through some change which would require extensive solar studies. The change on the earth might be the end life as we know it, but I am fairly certain that the sun has not changed." *They went to dinner where other experts were present.* The President said,

"We have an idea why the color yellow has disappeared and think the disappearance will be temporary. After this dinner, the crisis team will meet to discuss what has happened, and what course of action seems to be indicated. In the meantime, let us enjoy this wonderful meal which the chef has prepared for us. We welcome the wives; hope you can relax and enjoy the meal with us. Maybe tonight we can give you some good news as well as to the rest of the nation and the world." Aaron hugged his wife and said,

"Don't worry, we are going to solve this problem."

The meeting took several hours, but by 2 AM, the team agreed that Colonel Aaron Post was probably correct on the cause, and that it was probably temporary. The experts on the orbit of The Cloud agreed that it would cover half the world for about two months. They also agreed that the color yellow would return after July. Based on the sun radiation level received by the earth, the average temperature earth will drop by 20-30 degrees Fahrenheit. Remember Aaron said the June morning temperature was 45. The meteorologists hesitated to say how much this would affect the weather. They did say that we should prepare for very cold summer. They mentioned snow in the summer and probably a poor harvest. The effect would be minimized because this would only occur in June, July and August with a minor overlap in September.

The President sent the following recorded message to most Nations and went on nationwide television live. He said,

"For several months NASA has been following a large asteroid. It was forecast to miss the earth by 50 million miles, but for an unexplainable reason, it changed direction and should miss the earth by only 200,000 miles. On the morning of June 13th it unexpectedly exploded and scattered a fine dust along its path and perpendicular to the path. This resulted in a dust cloud between the sun and the earth. We have estimated that, based on The Cloud velocity, the color yellow should return in about 6-8 weeks. We expect average Earth's temperature will drop from 20 to 30 degrees Fahrenheit. The meteorologists estimate that this effect will last about 3-6 months. This means that some areas will be very cold even in the summer. There may be snow and ice in July and August. This is very serious because you may be exposed to low temperatures never seen in the middle latitudes since the ice age 12,000 years ago. Follow the local authority's directions until this situation clears. Do not take chances for it could be fatal." After the President's speech, Colonel Post said,

"Mr. President, I think we need to have a short meeting to discuss the possibility that humans or perhaps Aliens may have had a hand in this emergency. If so, why have we not been contacted by anyone for this attack? I don't think this was an accident."

"Why?"

"It is not normal for an asteroid to change direction and go between the earth and the sun and explode into a dust cloud. They have always gone around the sun, and exploding asteroids do not normally form dust clouds.

This event has the earmarks of human effort or maybe an Alien attack." If so, we are at war, and we don't know with whom or how bad it can get."

"We will have an early meeting tomorrow. Hell, I mean today. All of you are to be back here by 10:00 AM. Coronel Post has raised a question concerning responsibility for this occurrence. Get as much rest as you can but come prepared to discuss any espionage information that might bear on the subject. Put the CIA to work now. See you all at 10:00AM. Today." For clarity this is now June 14, 2110.

CHAPTER 2

THE MYSTERY DEEPENS

*Y*OU WILL RECALL THAT COLONEL Post had told *the President that this event with the disappearance of the color yellow and lower temperature, may have been an accident, but his opinion was that it was planned by some entity, either one of the world powers or an alien from another world.* President says,

"General Post, will start the meeting with his thoughts about the change in the sun's radiation. Ok General, it is your baby.

"What's this general stuff?"

"Didn't they tell you, I promoted you early this morning, and thought the general staff would give your stars? I just happen to have a couple; here, let me pin them on. Of course, you must be approved by the Senate to be permanent, but I don't think that will be any problem since you are well known by them." General Post says,

"Thank you, I appreciate the promotion. Gentlemen, there may be other ways to get world powers or the world's attention, but this one is brilliant and effective. It may also be the worse calamity to hit the earth since the dinosaurs were wiped out."

"General, you can't be serious; no country on earth would threaten the whole world with total destruction including themselves. You will need to give me more information if you expect me to believe such an idea."

"Sir, let us get the views of the panel. I suggest that we have each member state what information they have. Then we can sum it up and decide our course of action." The President says,

"You are right, go ahead." General Post says,

"I have a voice adapter for my computer, so each can use the microphone to record his or her information. My wife, Janice, can scan the information and summarize it on the computer. She does an excellent job and is quick. There is no one as fast and accurate as Janice. I think we should also have her in the meeting; it will speed things up later. Sir, please have the housekeeper bring her here immediately." *The President calls the housekeeper, and Janice arrives." Aaron gives his wife hug, and tells her that we are going to record the meeting.*

"We want you to listen to everything and summarize the information at the end of the meeting." She agrees to do it as quickly as possible. General Post starts the meeting with his contribution.

"From my observations, I am certain that the effect of lower temperatures and the loss of yellow are not a change in the sun, but the addition of the cloud or filter formed by the explosion of the asteroid in space between the sun and earth. The reason I think The Cloud is controlled by some entity is that an exploding asteroid goes around the sun, and does not usually form a cloud; as a matter of fact it is extremely rare. The other thing is that it gets the world's attention because it is extreme and uncontrolled by even the strongest country. It is quite cold this morning, a round 40 degrees Fahrenheit. I am sure The Cloud is responsible for the reduction of solar energy which we are receiving and the loss of the yellow color. I suppose that the sun could change in some way, but I doubt it. This change appears to be related to the dust cloud and not the sun. Since NASA has been observing this asteroid for several months, its change of direction, exploding and spreading to form a cloud, seem to indicate that we are being invaded by an alien from some other planet." The war has started, and we don't have a clue. The President says,

"Do you know what you just said? I can't tell the people that. There would be an uncontrolled panic. It is going to be bad enough just telling them that it is going to get colder. We can prepare the people for cold but never war at the same time." General Claassen,

"How do you fight a cloud? I know war tactics and how to fight, but this is completely out side of my training." General Post,

Well, General, we better find out damn quick because I think the casualties will quickly get horrendous, and there will be a panic, beyond our imagination." The President,

"Let's get back to the discussion; maybe we can determine if General Post is correct, and whether we can find a solution, or someway to meet this crisis, Patrick can tell us what NASA knows."

"Presently it appears to be moving at 66000 mph; it should pass out of the earth's area in about 5 months. We have not made any estimates of how cold it might get. If you will wait a few minutes, I will call the engineers to put the computer on the calculation, and they should have an answer in about an hour or perhaps less." General Post says,

"Before we can tell the people what the problem is and how long it will last, we will need those numbers. Thank you Patrick. Before you go, perhaps you should stay here to hear the numbers from NASA, the CIA and the Joint Chiefs. You will need a little ammunition. Charles Massy is here from CIA. Let us hear from Charley."

"Our information on all countries that might have the facilities to perform such a feat does not show evidence of preparing for the sudden drop in temperature. Perhaps Russia might be suspect because there appeared to be more than the usual activity at their missile site. I would discount this because NASA has been following this object for several months. Russia has never launched a deep space rocket except for an unmanned one for data search. We are continuing our information search, but at present we are unable to detect any earthly involvement. You know that the moon has sizeable USA, Russian and Chinese Units. We have not been able to contact any of them. Perhaps NASA can directly or thru the space station.

I am not familiar with their capability. Could one of them do such a project without being detected?" General Post says,

"I think they have the capacity to do about anything, maybe Claassen can tell us. Patrick see if NASA can resolve that communication problem soon,"

"Ok"

"I think we should hear from the Joint Chiefs representative. General Mike Claassen, let's hear from you."

"We also have not been able to contact our USA Unit, and we have asked NASA to try but no word yet. We are sure that anyone of the Units could manage a deep space project without detection, especially if they disabled the other two, or two of them cooperated and disabled the third one. Since they have been able to utilize He3, which is abundant in the moon soil, for power and since the raw materials are available; they can make whatever they desire and launch a ship. If NASA can't contact them, we plan to send a number of rockets with sufficient men and weapons to defend the USA Unit and to define the situation. It will take a week to get the rockets in place and ready to fire." General Post interrupts,

"General Claassen, you just said a week. Surely you can do that quicker. What is holding you up; this is war? We need information NOW!

"We can do it in 2 days and risk failure but I will go now and get it started. I guess I did not realize the urgency. I am familiar with war, but a cloud?"

"Good, we all have to realize that immediate planned activity is needed. We can't stall around. General, please finish what you were saying, then go."

"At the space station NASA has a large telescope which they could aim at the moon to assess the Unit's integrity or activities. We will have one ship ready to fly in two days to get a closer look, and land a large group to determine the status of the Units and defend the USA Unit. We will be in constant contact after the ship is launched. We can fix it, so that the conference room can communicate directly with the ship and the personnel who land on the moon. We will also keep a solder here at all times to listen, and call the conference members if something happens out of the ordinary. We will also record all transmissions for future reference. NASA have ascertained that The Cloud (1,000,000 miles long) would not completely surround the earth. As a matter of fact it would need to be 1,370,000 miles if it were to orbit and cover the earth. As soon as this meeting is completed, we need to provide information to all the services. They will need to move men and ships to a warmer climate. We can't have them frozen in ice." General Post says,

"Thank you General Claassen you have a busy job, and you should go now. The lack of contact with the moon further indicates Alien action. I think we will find Aliens on the moon. It appears we will have additional information, and we will want the sound connection here in the conference room. We will meet again when more information is available. Therefore all conference members will remain in Washington and available for a meeting on short notice. I just noticed that Patrick completed a phone call, and perhaps he has some answers to some of our questions. What do you know, Patrick?"

"We have the forecasted temperatures, and it is bad. In the summer, it looks as if it will approach 40 above and in the winter 40 below zero around the 40 degree north latitude. Maybe you would like to know how we calculated the numbers. I brought a sketch of the world with tangents to the world and the sun beam perpendicular to the earth between plus or minus 23.5 degrees latitude, the tilt to earth's orbit. You will note that beyond 23.5 the beam angle to the earth is the latitude minus 23.5 degrees NASA reports that ice is forming rapidly around the North Pole. Forecasting temperatures is a new experience for us. You need to remember these temperatures are only estimates and may change with time. NASA has not been able to communicate with the moon or use the telescope because the cloud is between the earth and moon. The moon should be clearly visible about midnight today when it moves away from behind the cloud. They will also try the telescope and radio communications when it is visible. We have also calculated how long the cloud will cover the earth. Based on the fact that The Cloud is traveling in the same direction as the earth is and is moving faster by about 500 mph, The Cloud will be with us for about 70 days. It appears that the effect of The Cloud will be minimized but will cover the Southern Hemisphere in 48 hours." General Post says,

"Patrick, that is welcome news, but we will certainly have a cold spell Ask NASA if they made any allowance for the fact, that The Cloud only covers the sun exposed side of the earth. It seems to me that night side would still radiate much the same as always which means it would get colder perhaps until the dew started forming. If I heard you correctly, you said the moon would pass thru The Cloud." Patrick says,

"We think that is possible for The Cloud to move out beyond the moon because it is travelling so fast. As its speed decreases, it will move inside the moon's orbit. So, we will see the moon pass through it twice." General Post says.

"We must contact the moon Unit, and maybe they can get a sample. We need to know its composition. The people can survive 10 above during this summer at 40 degree N latitude. I think we have enough information to say we are being invaded by an Alien force. What does The Cloud Committee say?"

"Yes, we agree." General Post says,

"We should talk about what we are going to do about the people. I have a few words to say about that.

When we measure the present sun radiation received by the earth, we can estimate future temperatures based our former summer and winter data. You will recall, that the reason for the change in seasons is a direct relationship to the fixed 23.5 degree tilt of the earth's axis to the plane of the earth's orbit. This causes sun to appear to move north and south of the equator 23.5 degrees each way for a total of 47 degrees. That is why we have winters, springs, summers and falls as earth's orbit changes the sun's incident angle. We can use the normal radiation numbers, the present measured sun's radiation and latitude to estimate the temperatures at other latitudes based on how much the suns radiation is spread by the latitude. This will give an average temperature, but the weather will probably control the actual one. It is winter in the Southern Hemisphere which means it will be much colder there than here. This also permits us to estimate summer and winter temperatures with The Cloud in place. I hope that NASA has some radiation numbers, so we can estimate how cold it might get at each latitude. Assuming that the sun's radiation is more or less constant between summer and winter, the only difference would be how the radiation is spread by the tilt of the earth's axis. At 40 degree latitude in our summer the spread is calculated on 40-23.5 or 16.5 degrees. In the winter the angle is 40 +23.5 or 63.5. The reason I am placing this first is that we must know how much colder it might get, and how long it might last, so we can prepare the people. This information will let us decide what to do about transportation of food, clothing, and how power is distributed. The second thing I would want to have determined is who are we fighting and what, if anything, do we do about the dust cloud. Before we start here is the agenda which I think we should cover. I welcome comments on the agenda, and we can change it if the group agrees." He hands a copy of the following list to each. Jeffery Banks, President assistant says,

"I visualize that the first part of this meeting will be to gather information, then discussion and assignment of responsibility. Additional meetings will be to report progress. General Claassen says,

"I have a suggestion on the agenda. I think the things that concern people should be discussed first. Items 8, 9 and 10 should replace items 4, 5 and 6." General Post says,

"We have corrected as the General suggested, and Janice has changed and printed a new copies and will give each a copy.

AGENDA TO DEAL WITH THE SUN'S CHANGE REVISED IIST

i. Determine the size of the emergency and how long is might last.

ii. What information do we need to inform the people?

iii. What can be done to help people survive the emergence?

iv. What about transportation and communications?

v. How do we handle food supplies?

vi. What will be the effect on electrical power and transmission lines?

vii. What can we do about people around the world?

viii. Is there anything we can do to reduce the effect of the dust cloud?

ix. What do we do about dead people and animals which will happen with the low temp?

x. Are we at war and with whom?

General Post says,

"We need to know how the temperatures might vary with latitude around the world. Although we do not have all the information, I think we have enough evidence for the President to call the larger Countries, and then have the state department call the rest to give them what information we have, so they can warn their people of the coming cold temperatures. I also suggest that the President interrupt this country's TV stations and give a warning directly to people. Also, give same information to each state government to get them to work protecting the people from the severe cold. He can also communicate any new developments. After the President is finished, the meeting will resume for we still have much to cover. Sir, we will take a break until you are finished." The President says to his assistant,

"Set up a television conference with the major countries, and any other countries you can contact. Tell me when it is ready. Also be sure there are interpreters because I will be speaking in English."

He interrupts the Television networks and says,

"It will get much colder; it may snow and stay on for several days, even in places that have never had snow. Get a supply of food for at least two months and then stay inside. Be sure you do not let children or pets outside. Most of you do not have adequate clothing for such low temperatures. Please do not get on the Main highways. We must keep them clear for food and military transport. We will set up an answering service on 24 hour duty to supply help and answers. We will broadcast the 800 number as soon as it can be set up. Also, watch your TV or listen to the radio which may answer your questions. We will have more information later. Gentlemen I have one more job to do. I am declaring a National State of Emergence and assigning the State Department the job of setting up the telephone service. It is up to them to do it even if necessary to recruit other departments except the Defense and Transportation. We must supply them information. I am also activating the State military Units to operate under martial law. Since the State Department Director is in this meeting, I suggest that you start now. We can do without you for some time; you may leave the meeting. The Director of Transportation, John Rison may also leave now. Ok General Post, you may get the meeting going again, Well wait, my assistant, says the computer conference is ready. You may come along and observe others reaction to the crisis." *Most of the group follows and listens while the President converses with the world leaders. There are varying results. All are wondering about the color change; some are becoming concerned with the change in temperature; some are just realizing that they have a serious problem, and others are in a panic. They all now realize that USA is already planning to define and solve the problem. He also tells all that the problem will only last for 70 days which is bad enough but at least not permanent.* General Post says,

"I suggest that we have a brief recess for the members to contact their families and to eat lunch. The meeting will reconvene at two thirty." President says,

"We will have lunch served in the conference room which means we can continue until it is brought to us."

He calls the housekeeper to bring a variety of sandwiches and drinks. He also tells all to make their calls and rest room visits. Patrick interrupts and says,

"The engineers just called me and said the previous information about The Cloud's direction and speed are incorrect. The Cloud appears to be going into orbit around the earth, is still spreading and slowing in the speed. The Cloud only covers the Northern Hemisphere and should completely surround it in 24 hours. It is also spreading to the Southern Hemisphere which will be covered in 48 hours. We estimate that The Cloud will be about ¼ its present thickness which means it should have less effect on filtering and earth temperatures." There was a groan from the committee. General Post says,

"Mr. President, in light of this new development, I suggest that we delay the meeting, until NASA can provide updated information. We can have a relaxing lunch and be refreshed for another session." President says,

"That is good idea. I will get the housekeeper to prepare lunch for the dining room. See you all in about 40 minutes." General Post says,

"We will cover the new information in the meeting after lunch. Patrick in the meantime try to get more details. This may change everything that we have told the people and other countries. In addition, estimate the length, and how much of the moon will be hidden. When will we be able to see the moon and for how long? We should not have been surprised that The Cloud would orbit, but I was too busy thinking about the people. It should have been obvious because it is inside the earth's zone of influence, 930,000 miles towards the sun. Of course, with the speed exceeding escape velocity, it should eventually leave the earth's orbit. Another thing, recalculate your temperature numbers. An orbiting cloud is going to be around a long time. The committee is free to leave. On second thought, I think we need to know at what distance from the earth The Cloud will orbit. The moons velocity is only 2300miles per hour and orbits at about 238000miles from the earth. It was previously reported The Cloud was moving at 66500miles per hour. Might this affect show how it would orbit? Would not the earth slow it some to ultimately determine the orbit path?" Patrick says,

"I agree, and it may be difficult to determine exactly where it will settle. I will get them working and report back when we have something to report." *General Post did not get a report from Patrick until after midnight. Patrick also said that he did not have a complete report. General Post called the committee members and told them the meeting would be at 9 am June 15th,*

While you are getting the data, I think we need to cover new item 5 and 6. I know that the Transportation Dept. only regulates, but you get the job of contacting trucking and railroads because you know who they are. You must get them and the unions to cooperate. Maybe you could get them together on a computer conference.

Distribution of food and clothing will be important. If you can't get them to co-operate, I think the President can declare an emergency and put the army in charge."

CHAPTER 3

PANIC SETS IN

JUNE 15, 2110 9AN

A BOUT 9 AM A GRIM *group had gathered in the conference room and were waiting for the President and General Post to arrive. They had already heard that NASA had confirmed that The Cloud appeared to be orbiting the earth which was depressing news. Although it was thinning, there was no increase in the radiation which meant the temperatures would continue to worsen. The President and General Post enter the room.* The President says,

"Ok General, you can get the Meeting started."

"I see by your faces, that you have heard the news about the orbiting cloud and no improvement in radiation as The Cloud thins. The situation is far worse than you can imagine. We have received some reports from around the world, and the temperatures from the winter half of the globe will get much worse than expected as The Cloud spreads. With The Cloud orbiting, things will not get better and will last much longer. Even the tropical areas will be quite cool. We are presented with an emergency for which we are totally unprepared to meet. We must consider what we can do and do it quickly. Our very lives, the infrastructure and the world survival depend on some temporary solution while we work on a permanent one. We need to define the habitable parts of the world; how transportation will work; how communications will work; how power transmission will work; how the people will be fed, and how will they be kept from freezing. The world is in twilight during the day, and most stars are invisible at night. The panic has begun in the Northern Hemisphere, even though we have told them that the summer will be no worse than a cold winter. Stores which supply food and clothing are overwhelmed. There have been numerous altercations, or perhaps riots would be a better word. The situation in USA is better, but we must gain control. The President has declared a state of emergency and activated the National Guard, but this is so wide spread, that I think they will have little effect. It is hard to believe, that we are so close to the primitive man. Oh yes, Janice has summarized our meeting from yesterday. Janice will hand out a copy to each of you. Hang on to this because we may get back to it if we survive. Before we begin a discussion, Patrick will give us the latest information. Patrick let us hear the words of terror."

"We know that The C loud will orbit the earth; it will completely surround the earth except the poles will be open, but the Southern Hemisphere will gradually close in 36 hours as The Cloud spreads south. Oh yes, there will be a vision of the moon inside The Cloud's orbit. We believe 'The Cloud will have an elliptical path, but we are not certain exactly where it will be. It appears that it may be outside the moon's orbit. It is slowing down some and its present speed is about 40000mph. This is above escape velocity, but it is slowing so fast, I think it will assume a fixed orbit inside the moon's orbit. It is still going away from the earth which means its speed will decrease some additional amount. According to our measurements, it is slowing faster than we expect from gravity alone. We are in the process of estimating the mean distance it will assume when in orbit. The engineers had to make an assumption about The Cloud motion because it is not a solid body to which the motion equations apply. You understand that we are doing some guessing and could be entirely wrong. We have the equations to calculate all the dimensions for fixed orbit of a solid body, but changing speed, direction and the dispersed parts of the rock requires estimates and multiple calculations to get a reasonable orbit estimate. The engineers are working on a solution and will call me when they know, but I don't think we will know what its orbit will be for a couple of days or so. I don't think that the temperature situation will get worse. Of course, it appears that the problem will last considerable longer no matter what the orbit becomes. We have estimated the temperatures for several latitudes by estimating how much the sun's radiation is spread as the latitude is increased." General Post says,

"A close approximation for spread area is given by the formula H = A divided by the cosine of the Latitude -23 for summer or the cosine of the latitude +47 for winter. H is the radiation incident area and A is the perpendicular incident area. Anyone who wants to see the details can see them in Patrick's office. From this NASA is making a chart showing the temperatures as the latitude changes. You realize that these are only estimates of the average. Depending on the weather, the actual temperature may be much different for some areas and times." Patrick says,

"We were requested to communicate with the moon. We have tried several times but were unable to get any answer. We also viewed the three units with the space station telescope several minutes at various times. We frequently observed visible actions before The Cloud came but none afterward. It was almost as if there were no one on the moon. My phone is ringing." He answers and says,

""NASA says the moon is passing through the tail of the cloud; go outside, you will be surprised." They all rush outside and the moon is about half way though The Cloud. The portion in contact with The Cloud is shooting off sparks similar to several very large roman candles. General Post is the first to recover,

"Well!, that is quite a sight. Do you think the moon will be the same? This may make space travel a little more dangerous. The Cloud appears to be electrically charged and also controlled by powers we don't yet understand based on The Cloud changing speed and this pyrotechnical display. This is more evidence, that we are being attacked by Aliens. We have much to learn, but the effects on earth comes first. Let's get back to the meeting, and determine what we can do now." Everyone proceeds to the conference room. On the way back, Janice clutches Aaron's arm and says,

"I know you so well; you are planning to do something." He smiles,

"Honey, I am covered up with the people job; when that gets going, I can sit down and give The Cloud problem my attention. This is so big, that I know I must decide with your help. I shall not keep you in the dark. Please be patient. Let us get this meeting going. Ok honey?"

"Yes, I love you. Who would have thought the lack of yellow could cause so much trouble?" General Post says,

"Sometimes a little thing can escalate into a big problems. Mr. President I don't want you lie to the people, but I sure would want you to say something to calm them down. We can't help them if they are going to riot. They will tear down the infrastructure. We need them to be cooperative. I suggest you get back on the TV and give them reasons to trust us, and to know that we will solve the problem. Another thing, we must warn the Southern Hemisphere about the really cold temperatures which will hit in 24 hours. As soon as you complete your TV talk, we will discuss the Southern problem." The President interrupts the TV programs and says,

"We think we have a solution, but the next two, or so months will not be worse than the worse winter you have ever experienced. You have easily survived the worst, and you can again. Food may be in short supply, and that could make things tough, but a few of you need to lose a little weight. It could be good for all of us to know a little privation, and know we can survive. Plan to limit your food consumption. We have enough food to last for about one year or more without growing any if you don't try to hoard food and clothing. Remember when the going gets tough, the people of USA know how to get going. The transportation system is capable of moving food, clothing and materials under the conditions we are forecasting. The supply of gas, gasoline and electrical power should be adequate. Other countries may have bigger problems, but we have not decided how to help them. The Southern Hemisphere has winter already; it will be much worse and will require our help very soon. General Post you may start the meeting."

"We need to warn the Southern Hemisphere about the coming cold temperatures. What can we tell them about how to stay warm, anybody?" Admiral Perry says,

"My son is a mining engineer, and he says that deep mines get quite warm. It seems to me that if people used the mines and took food with them, they would survive until we worked out a permanent solution." General Post says,

"That is a wonderful. Idea, but how do we convince them that we are right. They would need to do it immediately not tomorrow. We are talking about millions of people who would need to move. I think it is impossible." John Rison says,

"It has never been done before, but maybe it will help at least for a few who make the effort, and we might save more than we think. Creating a panic is not the way, but it may be the only way. Although we do not have the chart of temperatures, we know it will be a killing cold. I think the State Dept. should contact the Southern Hemisphere immediately with what information we have now." *The President calls the State Dept. and puts emphasis on the need for haste, and how quickly the people must move to deep minds or caves. He also says we will contact the State Dept. when we have more information. General Post says,*

"I see that John Rison has returned. Let's hear about transportation." John says.

"Trucking, railroads and the unions agreed that this cold weather created an emergency which they would do their best to meet. They will work overtime without overtime pay and will move materials, food and clothing to the places which need them. They will maintain schedules but do emergency deliveries as required. They said that they do this all the time and know how to keep the process going. The oil industry said that they do not have a problem with the low temperatures, but a blizzard might hold them up some. They said that the Alaskan production would cease if it got much colder, but they could make up the difference in the Gulf because the temperature probably would not get much below freezing." General Post says,

"That is good news. Maybe when the people see the trucks moving, they will calm a little. General Claassen, where do we stand on the trip to the moon? I don't think you will be going through The Cloud because its orbit is beyond the moon's. I want a sample of The Cloud, but I don't want to risk your mission. When will your ship jump off?"

"The first ship will take off tomorrow, June 16th. They will avoid The Cloud because we can fly over the top if necessary. The Cloud is only about 5000 miles wide now. Even if it is between the earth and the moon, there is plenty of space to avoid it. Their average speed will be 25000 mph which will take about 10 hours to complete the trip." General Post says,

"If the moon is obscured from our sight, I suspect that radio transmissions will not pass through The Cloud. I believe we can get some information through the space station. You know that the space station is 4000 miles above the earth and is in a polar orbit which will put it in line of sight of the moon about half of time and will not depend on the moon's orbit. We should get most of the information." General Claassen says,

"We will make arrangements with NASA to handle our transmissions, so that they are broadcast to the conference room." General Post says,

"I see Marilyn Linden from the State Dept. has returned. Have you be able to set up the 800 line?"

"Yes but it was overwhelmed, and I don't think that it is very efficient. I would like to make a suggestion."

"Implement whatever plan you think will work. You have complete authority to do it the best you know how. We are going to be too busy to listen to your plan. If you run into a problem you can't solve, we will look at it. You are free to go, and we will feed you information as it develops. Gentlemen, we seem to have taken care of United States at least temporarily. General Claassen, I assume you have already moved the armed services or told them to move to the south. Is that correct?"

"Yes. We are still working on how they will be located, but they have been told to move south of 40 degrees north latitude. You know the recent opening of the new Canal through Nicaragua will easily handle any size ship. Therefore we can move ships between the Atlantic and Pacific." General Post says,

"We have already told them about the caves. I have some ideas about helping the people in the Southern Hemisphere. I want the committee to think about the problem and come up with some suggestions. They will be really hurting. Some will think they will not be hit, but The Cloud will cover them soon causing lower temperatures. I just looked at the globe; most of the land mass is north of the 45 degree south latitude. I think if they move their people toward the equator; they will survive at least until we can get a permanent solution. Also they must get warmer clothes and food. Do you agree with that suggestion? What say you?" The group all say yes to that idea. General Post says,

"Mr. President, maybe you should get the State Dept. to contact those southern countries again with our suggestions."

The President calls the State Dept. and tells them they have a priority job to contact all countries in the Southern Hemisphere, and urge them to move people toward the equator where it will be warmer. Also they must get the transportation service to cooperate. We will contact you when we have a permanent solution.

"General, let us continue the meeting." General Post says,

"The Northern Hemisphere has considerable land and population north of the 45 degree north latitude. Although it is summer, that area will get quite cold. So that is the problem for now. Can we help them and if we can, how? Or should we turn our attention to The Cloud?" General Claassen says,

"I think we should give them the information we have and ask them if they need any help. If it is going to get 40 degrees Fahrenheit at 40 degree latitude, all of Canada, Alaska, and most of Europe will be frigid, and northern Africa will be quite cold. You know that the Gulf Stream helps Western Europe. As a matter of fact the coast of Norway is completely free of ice the year around. I thought Patrick was making a chart of temperatures by latitude. Patrick, where is your damned chart? You know we could have had some real numbers by now. Do we have some real numbers? Patrick says,

"As a matter of fact we have real numbers from the weather bureau. They are not as low as the calculated numbers, but it has only been a couple of days since The Cloud. The chart was ready and I looked at it but forgot to bring it. I see Harry, one of the engineers, bringing it in to the Conference room." General Post says,

"I see the temperature chart has arrived. We can discuss it now and then discuss what we can do to help other countries. Can we have the chart taped to that board, so we can all see it."

"Yes, just a minute." General Post says,

"At first glance, the temperatures from the Canadian border to northern edge of South America will be livable but uncomfortable for the summer. It would seem that USA will be ok, but above the 60 degree latitude it will be very cold. The Canadians need to move south to below the 60 degree latitude where they will be able to survive. South of the equator it will get extremely cold for it is winter there. I don't believe the majority of people can survive unless we can solve The Cloud problem quickly. Telling them to move north was a bad idea. Mr. President please contact the State Dept., and cancel that job we just gave them."

"That is an excellent suggestion." He calls and finds that they have not made the calls. He tells them not to make the calls, and that they will receive further instructions later." General Post says, o TEMPERATURES BY LATITUDE BASED ON READINGS AT 40 LATITUDE

Actual Latitude	Calculated Latitude	Calculated Temperature	Calculated Cosine
90	67	-255F	
80	57	-175F	.544
70	47	-103F	.682
60	37	-42F	.798
50	27	06F	.891
40 Basis	17	40F	.956
30	07	58F	.002
23SunPos	00	68F	1.000
20	-03	61F	-0.998
10	-13	59F	-0.974
00Equator	-23	22F	-0.920
S10	-33	-21F	-0.899
S20	-43	-77F	-0.731
S30	-53	-146F	--0.602
40	-73	-253	-0.503

"Sometimes our mistakes do not catch us. We must have our facts straight before we leap. I think their survival depends on staying where they are for a longer time. China will be cold, but it is mostly south of the 45 latitude. India and Africa north of the 10 N degree latitude will be cold but livable. Of course the mountain range on the north side of India will be very frigid. Any life south of the 10 degree South Latitude may not survive very long. Let us discuss the problem south of the equator. You know we may have missed lunch. Mr. President please get your assistant to have sandwiches and drinks brought to Conference Room while we discuss this frigid topic." John Harris, from Weather says,

"We have not yet seen these low temperatures. On the average they are about 75 degrees warmer but we agree they will get lower as your calculations indicate and The Cloud spreads south." General Claassen says,

"We have the whole navy powered by nuclear energy. We can move a lot of material and maybe people, but if we can avoid moving people, we might have less chaos." General Post says,

"Good, but I don't think clothing will help much. I think they need energy as well as clothing. Let us hear some more ideas."

John Rison says,

"When I was talking to the transportation people, they suggested several winter clothing manufactures which I should contact. I called them, and they agreed to speed up the process. We could move more clothing to the colder regions with the navy ships." General Post says,

"I think that will take too much time, but it may be useful later If we can keep them from freezing now. Admiral Jason Perry says,

"We have mentioned caves and mines and gave them the suggestion. Perhaps we should repeat and recommend a large supply of food and drinkable water there." General Post says,

"That is the best idea so far. Perhaps if we contact each country, maybe they might have their own ideas, especially when we tell them what the temperatures will reach. Also, we should suggest that each person take his own food and water for at least 2 weeks, some food which will not spoil. Maybe by that time we will have solved The Cloud problem, or we can deliver food, water and winter clothing. If they can give us a map of mines and caves locations, we could drop supplies every couple of weeks. It looks as if the State Department may get much larger to handle the communications. Do we all agree this is the best way to handle south of the equator?" All agreed. General Post says,

"General Claassen, I think contacting each government and arranging for help should be your job and not the State Dept. responsibility. Just appoint a General to the job, so we can get on with the Northern Hemisphere. We excuse you for the time needed to get the leader appointed. When you get back, we will update you. I suppose that the cave and mine solution would work in the Northern Hemisphere at least for some areas such as Russia. I am thinking about what General Claassen said about the Gulf Stream. Do you suppose the temperature could be increased some and thus moderate the European climate?"

"A chorus of voices drowned him out." When it died down, General Post said,

"I agree it seems wild, but if you have a better idea, I will forget that I mention it. My intention was to get you thinking about ideas, such as supplying energy. Well, what say you?" Things got quiet for a while and the General went for a walk with his wife. What they talked about, we will never know. In about 2 hours they returned. General Claassen said,

"The group has decided to explore your idea. We think, you should make an estimate of how much energy might be needed to raise the temperature one degree Fahrenheit, and how you would get the energy into the Gulf Stream. In other words, you must determine feasibility, and we think you must have the answer by tomorrow afternoon. We are giving you 24 hours." General Post said,

"I don't think that I will need 24 hours after you hear what I have to say. While we were walking my wife said,"

"They were awfully quiet when we left. They are either discussing another idea or yours. When we return, you will need some answers if they choose your idea." General Post said,

"We then went to library and looked up a few facts about the Gulf Stream. It is about 40 miles wide, several hundred feet deep and moving at about 5.5 miles per hour, but I decided that we would only be interested in the top 10 or so feet. If we warmed the top 10 ft. of the water, it will be lighter and float on the top which is where we want it to be, so the wind will be warmed before it flows over Europe. I won't go thru the calculations, but it turns out that for the volume I have described, it will take 850 million kilowatt-hours to raise the temperature one degree Fahrenheit. If we raise the temperature 10degrees F, we could pump a lot of energy into the air. That is a lot but feasible with nuclear power provided by our navy. I don't know any details about how it could be done. Therefore, we need the services of a Nuclear Engineer and

Oceanographer. The first is to tell us how and supervise the process. The second will tell us where to add the heat. General Claassen, What do you have to report?"

"I have appointed General Maitland for the Southern Hemisphere and outlined the job for him. He will give us progress reports."

"Thank you General Claassen. You have Nuclear Engineers in the Navy. I want the best, and the one who will not let anything stand in his way. I know an Oceanographer and will call him as soon as I leave this meeting. Have I convinced you that the idea is worth following up?" A chorus of voices agree.

"Yes, the food has arrived." General Post says,

"Let's stop and eat our late lunch and then discuss what we will tell the Northern Hemisphere. It is four PM; I think we should take a break and return at 6:00PM. General Claassen don't forget to have that Nuclear Engineer here by noon tomorrow even if you must fly him. I will have the Oceanographer here also." They eat lunch and return at 6PM

CHAPTER 4

IS THIS THE NEW ICE AGE

G ENERAL POST SAYS,

"We have given the best advice for the Southern Hemisphere, unless you have thought of any other suggestions. Anyone? Well, I guess we will consider the problem for the Northern hemisphere. Before we start, I have reviewed our Navy's Nuclear power. Our ships have much larger power systems than necessary for the speeds and weapons we had when they were built. Their present extra power is theoretically 500,000,000 to 1,000,000,000 Kilowatt hours per ship. Each ship's power is sufficient to increase the Gulf Stream temperature by ½ to 1 degree or more. I feel better about the possibility of accomplishing the task. We must thank the Navy for being farsighted in countering the Chinese with the powerful laser ability. The USA ships of today require lots of power to drive them at high speeds and to operate the laser beams; a position the Chinese have not attained yet.

Tomorrow at noon or so we will have the personnel to man the European project. Patrick, do you have any more information about The Cloud?"

"Yes, the speed of The Cloud appears to be slowing more than expected. If it continues reducing at this rate, we expect the orbit to be around 160,000 miles radius. If this happens, The Cloud will thicken slightly which means some reduction in the solar radiation received. We have also noticed that the moon left two holes in The Cloud which are persisting. We are also puzzled by a small spot in The Cloud which appeared solid. The engineers have not been able to decide whether it is a piece of un-shattered rock or something else. It appears more uniform than one might expect a rock to be." General Post,

"Have you looked at it in other parts of the spectrum?"

"No, but we are setting up to do that and should have an answer tomorrow or the next day."

"What do you mean by uniform?"

"Whatever it is; it is very regular in shape."

"Can you get a picture of it"

"We will have it tomorrow." General Post says,

"That information may be important. I have some thoughts about sending a mission to The Cloud. There are certain things we need to know before sending a person. We do not want to risk a person without knowing what the risk is. So get all the information you can. After we have given our information and recommendations to the Northern hemisphere, we will discuss missions. Ok, gentlemen what are we going to impart to the Northern hemisphere? I think we have generally agreed to the following list and Janice will past out a copy to each of you."

1. All should move south of 60 degree latitude or find a deep cave or mine in which they can survive for 6 months. This includes food, water and clothing. You will be exposed to minus 200+ degrees Fahrenheit on the surface.
2. Those south of the 60 degree latitude will need winter clothing, a warm shelter and access to food for 6 months.
3. Those between 50 and 30 degrees north latitude will see cold temperatures to the north with somewhat higher temperatures to the south. The weather systems could drastically change this, but no worse than the coldest of winters. Be sure you check the weather daily and have food available for two weeks. If the weather forecast is for extreme cold weather, you may need more food and winter clothing.
4. Those between 10 and 30 north latitude will be warmer but still much cooler than normal. You will need some warmer clothing. Have food for 10days. You will probably need heat or several blankets where you are living.
5. Those south of 10 degrees south should stay where you are and try to stay warm unless you can get in a deep mine and have food and water. The equator temp will be about 22 degrees Fahrenheit which is quite cold and below freezing.

6. Those countries who receive most of their food from ships must decide how they can feed the people. We will help where we can.

General Post says,

"Send this information to all countries between 10degree north latitude to 90 degrees north latitude. Also include a chart showing the temperatures by latitude and some cities because most people don't use latitudes to describe location. In addition, tell the European countries that we think we can raise the temperature of the Gulf Stream about 10 degrees Fahrenheit. If we get a consensus, we will make the effort; if not, we will abandon attempting to heat the Gulf Stream. You know that the Gulf Stream warms northern Europe. We have ascertained that there is a viable chance that the Gulf Stream can be warmed several degrees. We have the nuclear power in our Navy available if it can be utilized. We suppose that it is possible it might change the weather, but you are going to get a change if that The Cloud stays around. It now appears that it will orbit the earth at 160,000 miles radius. Unless the world can get rid of The Cloud, it appears that we could have it for an indefinite time, maybe too long to survive. Have the State Dept. send to European countries and Asian coutries." Patrick says,

"We have been unable to communicate with the three powers located on the moon with the space station, with or without the cloud in between. We have viewed the moon units with a telescope and we see no activity which was previously evident." General Claassen says,

"On June 16th we will launch a military rocket with a group to ascertain the state of all forces there. We will be in constant contact with the rocket thru the trip and the landing. We will keep you apprised of the results." General Post says,

"We suggest that European countries immediately look at the supply of food and clothing; how they are handled, and do whatever they must do to prevent hoarding. We will do whatever we can to help. If you need help, send a message to the President; we will have them read and prioritized. Is there any more information we should send?" John Rison, from transportation says,

"I think it would be well to give more information to them about food and clothing. It seems to me that a lot of their supplies are shipped in. Some may have supply problems." General Post says,

"Good suggestion, I will add to the message. Are there any other suggestions? No. Marilyn, I see you have returned. Did your plan work?"

"Very well, and so far we have had few complaints."

"Did you get the Southern Hemisphere the information about caves and mines?"

"Yes, but they did not seem to be accepting our advice. I think they expect us to do more. I said they should move rapidly because the really cold temperatures would arrive in 24 hours. I advised them to help themselves, and that we are doing all we can to get rid of The Cloud."

"You showed initiative, and I am proud of you. I have another job for you. We have written a memo to send to the Northern Hemisphere countries. Janice will give you a copy. Please get it off as quickly as possible. We are going to discuss a mission to The Cloud tonight and tomorrow how to heat the Gulf Stream. You should sit in tomorrow's noon meeting. Thanks for your help."

"Don't worry; the message will go tonight. See you tomorrow." General Post says,

"I would like to discuss missions to The Cloud with the President, General Claassen, Patrick Bartell and Janice. She is a former French Astronaut and is very good at analyzing projects. She has actually flown, and I have not. The first item would be to send an instrumented probe to assess the problem, and the precautions to take for a manned flight. Can a probe assess the atmosphere inside as well as outside the probe for electrical hazards? We seem to have problems with radio reception with The Cloud around which prevents monitoring it remotely. Perhaps we could preprogram it, so that it would automatically return. What would happen to a space suit if we needed to go outside? What effect would the dust cloud have on a space ship? How soon can we send a probe, and how long would it take before it could be returned? There may be other questions, but it seems to me we need these answers before a human gets involved." The President says,

"You don't need me, if is money, don't be concerned. Whatever it takes, I think Congress will go along. The House leader, Frank Harrison and the Senate leader, Jan Pearson have been here and have seen and heard what is happening. I assume the two of you will not hold up what we think necessary; will you?"

"Mr. President, we will support your decisions. Just let us know what the price will be to save us all. We hope we don't need to dig too deep." The President says,

"I and the Congress Representatives will see you all tomorrow at noon." General Post says,

"We will see you tomorrow. It is now 8PM. Do you think we can get this mission planning finished by 10 PM? I am sure we need some rest. If not, I suggest that we meet at 9 AM tomorrow morning." Patrick says,

"I knew this would come up. I have discussed the subject with the engineers, and they think we have sufficient equipment to assemble a probe with everything you have mentioned plus some additional testing items. They think the probe could be fired off tomorrow afternoon. The delay is mainly waiting for General Claassen's ship to leave. The probe could reach The Cloud in 4 or 5 hours, fly around in The Cloud for 5 hours and return to earth for a soft landing in about another 10 hours. In other words we could have the results by early on the 17th." General Post says,

"Well, that sounds great. Have you got the human probe figured out also?"

"We thought about it but decided that you might want to participate, but we do have a ship that will be available after June 18th. But I am sure some delay will occur based on the instrumented probe results."

"Well, meet me tomorrow at 8 AM June 16 at NASA, so we can agree on the probe instrumentation. Then it can be sent off in the afternoon.

"You have moved my estimate up several days. Let us call it a day, so we can spend some time with our families. Janice and I will be at NASA tomorrow morning, and we will need to change the meeting time to 11:30AM. See you tomorrow. Come on Janice, let's go."

"I knew you were going to fly up there. I was a French astronaut, so I know what it is. I could feel it my bones. Well, you are not going alone. It is me. Me. me."

"Don't worry; I had no intention of doing it without you. I am crazy about you, and I would not leave you out because you have better communication skills. We are a team forever."

CHAPTER 5

PLANS AND CHANGING PLANS

G ENERAL POST SAYS,
"I see that all the members of the special Cloud Committee are present. Before we get into the discussion of the Gulf Stream, I know you all want to hear about the meeting that Janice and I had with NASA this morning. As Patrick told you last night, they were ready to send a probe. After we discussed the instrumentation, it was agreed that the probe would be sent off this afternoon after General Claassen's ship departed. The probe is scheduled to return tomorrow. When we have the noon meeting on the 18th, we should have a few answers and a picture of the object in The Cloud. This Cloud thing keeps giving us new mysteries. You all probably watched on TV the ships taking off this morning for the moon. General Claassen, bring us up to date. Since they have been on the

way for about 5 hours, we should have heard from them in this conference room."

"We have attempted to contact them several times in the last hour through our system and NASA's, but at this time there has been no reply. We will try to contact hem at regular intervals. NASA has been observing them on their telescope, and there appears to be no obvious problem. They are on track. I have no idea why communications have failed. It could be some temporary glitch, or maybe The Cloud has powers beyond our knowledge." General Post says,

"Do what you can, and we will hope that it is only a temporary glitch. But, I tend to agree with your second idea because NASA has programmed the probe to return automatically. They and we thought that communications might not work. We will check how well communications works but will not rely on it. There is little we can do now. Let us get on with the Gulf Stream proposition. I see there are two new people in the room. I will introduce the oceanographer, Henry Jenson. Come here Henry; maybe after you hear our crazy idea, you can be a help. General Claassen, introduce the nuclear power engineer."

"I know Harold Wilson is totally bewildered because he was snatched from his job with no explanation, and I have not had time to explain. Well, Harold you will hear what it is about now, but essentiality it is to heat a very large quantity of water with nuclear power. I will let General Post explain since it was his idea."

"It is a well-known fact that Europe is warmer because the Gulf Stream flows toward Europe. It is sufficient to keep the Norway shore line free of ice during the winter. You probably noticed that the sun has dimmed, and it is quite cool in our summer, but it will be frigid during the winter. As you know, the Southern Hemisphere is having winter now. This is caused by a particle cloud which is expected to completely surround the earth, and cause the earth to become colder. Unless we can remove The Cloud, the earth may become uninhabitable for all warm blooded species. We are taking steps to temporarily save as many species as possible while we determine how to remove The Cloud or its effect. One of these is heating the air which normally moves from the west across Europe. Since we know that maybe we can heat the Gulf Stream sufficiently to prevent very low temperatures, perhaps some European temperatures will be no lower than a normal winter. I have information, that our nuclear powered ships have enough power to increase the Gulf Stream temperature about 10 degrees F. I propose to heat a stream of water 40 miles wide, 10 feet deep and moving at about 5 miles/hour. I have two questions, can we utilize the Navy's nuclear power, and where should we place the ships? I realize you can't immediately answer these questions. We have some time because Europe has not yet agreed to let us try. You realize; that even if we have the ok, it will take 50 hours to get the ships in place. We will give you 10 hours to answer the question of feasibility, placement of ships and delay time for modifications, if needed. I propose that we start getting the ships in place within the next 40 hours with our best guess now. This means when Henry is ready to give his best location, we will have started the process. If Harold thinks the ships need some modification, we will still move ships to Henrys specific location and the modifications will be done on site. The raw construction materials will be moved there by fast torpedo boats. Is that ok Admiral Perry."

"Yes, we can meet whatever schedule you set up."

"Time is our enemy; I can't emphasis how' much. Our survival may depend on your answers at least for Europe. Your 10 hours starts now. If you have questions, we will attempt to answer them. We want your best answer in 10 hours not the perfect answer. I suggest you find a quiet place, perhaps the library, while we continue this meeting. We will expect you back at 9:30 PM. You are excused. Gentlemen while I was trying to sleep, some other problems popped up. There are a few farm animals on which we depend, and they also must survive. Do we need to also protect food and flower seeds from extreme cold? We need some experts in these two fields. Perhaps the Agriculture Department could give us an answer or lead to the experts. Marilyn, How about taking on another job? I know we are loading you up, but I bet you have an assistant who can keep the State Department running while you are on special assignment"

"Yes, go on."

"I think the group would agree we need information about animals and seeds upon which we depend on for food. You can start with Ag Dept. to determine what protection may be needed to assure that the future food supply is still here after The Cloud is removed. The supply will be much larger when we consider what may happen in the Southern Hemisphere. Get back to us as soon as possible with a plan backed by concrete information. I guess that is all for now. I know you will do your best. You may go."

"I will be back as soon as I can." General Post says,

"Although I like to do the Gulf Stream heating project, I am beginning to think that Europe will survive, at least in the summer time, without heating the Gulf Stream. What is happening in the Southern hemisphere is far more serious. People, animals and vegetation will be subjected to killing cold weather. Is there anything we can do to ameliorate the pending conditions?" General Claassen says,

"If we give up on the Gulf Stream project, we still have all that nuclear power. But, that only has limited use and would do little for the whole hemisphere. You are asking for something that would retard the earth's radiation, and therefore keep them warmer. I recall that in the past there was some work done to reduce the upper air reflection of heat energy from the earth. Perhaps they also found something to increase it. An online search would be a good place to start." John Harris, weather officer comments,

"A hundred years ago the world was greatly concerned with the world getting too hot because the atmosphere was reflecting too much energy. It was believed that the industrial world released too much of certain chemicals which stayed in the upper atmosphere and was transparent to the sun's radiation but not the earth's lower frequency radiation (heat). Hence the earth's temperature would rise to intolerable levels. The oceans would rise; the people would need to move north; crops would move north; deserts would occupy more of the earth; tropical diseases would be rampaging, and some islands and cities would disappear in the water. Some of these gases were chlorine, carbon dioxide, carbon monoxide and some refrigerants. No one has ever proved that it was going to get hotter, but we still have windmills, electric cars and solar energy. The use of coal almost disappeared. None of the hot weather has happened, and it nearly bankrupted the nation. One should never give politicians something new to worry about. They generally get it all screwed up and think they have a reason to increase the taxes. The oil is still coming despite the forecasts of its demise. If oil disappears or becomes expensive, we can always make it with our cheap Nuclear Power. Of course, we still have rockets spewing gases which no one seems to mind. Perhaps we could increase the reflecting of the upper atmosphere, but who wants that around if The Cloud is dissipated. I, for one, am against messing with the upper atmosphere because you may get nothing, but on the other you might get something far worse than The Cloud." General Post says,

"Well John, I am not sorry that we turned you on. Out of controversy some good ideas generally develop. What happens if we can't get rid of The Cloud? I think messing the upper atmosphere should stay on the list. I agree with your opinion if we can dream up any other solution. Well, gentlemen, what====? Marilyn, I thought you left."

"No, I stepped outside and called the Ag Dept. They agreed to contact some specialists immediately and would get back to me soon. I came back because I wanted to know what was happening. I have a suggestion. If you were going to heat air west of Europe, would it be possible to heat the air in the Southern Hemisphere along some of the coastline. The weather dept. would know the prevailing winds for each country. Perhaps we could save some portion of the Southern Hemisphere." General Post says,

"That is good Idea. We will add it to list. John, do you have prevailing wind charts?"

"Yes, I will get the office to run some copies. I will call the assistant manager now to be sure they are delivered as quickly as possible. I have a suggestion. In some of the factories, I have seen some very large fans, at least 10 ft. in diameter or more. Perhaps they could be rigged to provide a wind. You know that many of the cities are on or near the shore line in South America. Ships could probably dock in some harbors. Do you suppose that the Navy knows which harbors are navigable?" General Post says,

"All in favor of abandoning the Gulf Stream project temporarily raise your right arm. I see we have 100% agreement. Patrick will you go to the library and bring Henry and Harold back here?"

"Yes" He leaves at a trot.

"Admiral Perry, we need those charts showing the navigable harbors and streams. Perhaps you could contact the right people to obtain them."

"Yes, I would be glad to do that immediately. We can expect to have the charts by the meeting time tomorrow (June 17)"

"We will also need a list of all of the nuclear driven ships showing their draft depth, beam clearance and power available for using."

"Yes, we will get that also."

"I also want to find out about fans, but let us have a short break while we wait for Patrick to return." Patrick, Henry and Harold return as well as the other members. General Post says,

"We have decided to temporarily abandon the Gulf Stream project for now and try to help the Southern Hemisphere. Europe should be able to survive at least for the summer, but the Southern Hemisphere will not.

That Hemisphere will suffer much more in its winter. We are investigating heating the air at some locations with the Navy's nuclear power. Perhaps we can save a portion of that area. Henry you may be some help in placement of ships, but I suspect that the location will be determined by where the air needs the heat. Harold you are going to figure how we can get the energy into the air for each location. I am almost sure that fans will be a part of the hardware. Does anyone here know about fans, sizes, power and air flow capacity?" Harold says,

"I have some experience, but I am not an expert. I know a woman with whom I worked a few years back."

"Can you get her here by noon tomorrow? We will pay air fare or send a plane to pick her up."

"Yes, I think I can. I have not seen her for 6 months. I have been conducting a long distance courtship on the phone and e-mail. I wish that project would prosper."

"How about calling her now? GO!"

"I am going; this is a great opportunity to improve my chances."

"Tell her we will send the President's plane to pick her up. Mr. President is that ok, sir?

"Yes, we don't have time for commercial operations."

"Thank you for backing me up. Find out which airport is nearest; how far she is from it, and we will also send a car to pick her up. Tell her that she will be staying at the White House and to pack warm clothes." *Harold goes out in the hall and makes the call. He dashes back in saying,*

"I have her on the phone, but she does not believe me. She knows that I am pushy." The President says,

"Give me the phone; I am good at giving orders. What is her name?"

"It is Sherry Jennings."

"Miss Jennings, this is the President of United States. You have probably noticed that the sun has dimmed, and that it is getting cooler. This is caused by a cloud between the sun and earth. Although we are colder, the Southern Hemisphere will be much colder because it is already winter there. We have been discussing using fans and heat to circulate warm air over some cities. You are an expert on fans from what Harold said. We need you to be a member of The Cloud Committee working to help those who will be suffering minus 200 degrees F. We don't have time to wait. Get you bag packed! As soon as you tell us the nearest Commercial Airport, we will send my plane to bring you to Washington." She replies,

"I live in Dallas, and I can be at the airport in one hour."

"Don't do that; give me your address, and we will send a car. You don't want to leave your car at the airport since you will not know when you will return. Besides that, you will have time to pack. Give me your Employer's name, and we will tell them why you were snatched away. The car will pick you up in an hour and half, and the plane will leave here in 30 minutes. Sound ok." She says,

"Yes, I will be ready and gives her address and her Employer's telephone number. I did not realize that Washington could move so fast, goodbye."

"We can when the need arises, goodbye." General Post says.

"Last night when I could not sleep, I just happen to have one of my old engineering books. It had a small chapter on fans and listed sizes and air flow capacity for some fans. I took a city the size of 40 square miles. an estimated a wind velocity of 15mph and a depth of 5000ft to estimate the cubic feet/min moving over the city, I wished to get some idea of the job magnitude. If all these numbers are converted to feet and minutes, it turns out that two fans of 120000 cfm capacity would be enough to move as much air as a 15mph wind would move over a 40 mile wide city. I know you visualize something big, but the fan is only 8 ft. in diameter. The thing that bothers me is that air flow from a fan may not spread much horizontally. In the air stream, two fans would be at least 10 miles apart. I hope this fan engineer can come up with a solution.

Janice, I hope you are taking these questions down; for I have several more."

"Yes I am taking them down."

"What temperature does the fan air need to be? It seems to me that if the temperature were too high, the air would rise too high to do any good. What criteria will determine which areas we should try to save? Will ice form in the ocean and streams to inhibit movement of ships? Should we be heating the ocean or streams in strategic locations? Would heating the oceans and streams do a better job of warming the land areas? Maybe we could heat the ocean enough to prevent freezing and the air to keep the land area warmer. It seems to me that the air would require less energy than the oceans. How long will it take to get the fans, heat exchangers and the ships ready to go? Harold can you answer any of these questions?"

"Yes, I have some opinions. There are pipes against the outside of the ships surfaces which are used to facilitate moving through some icing conditions. We would need heat exchanges with the fans to heat the air. We can estimate the temperature required to prevent the air from rising more than a specified height. We will need to specify that height. This may affect the number of fans and heat exchangers. Of course, other factors may determine the number of fans, ships and exchangers. You must know that the fan exhaust even at 50 mph will not extend to 20 miles. It seems to me that we will depend on the wind to distribute the warm air. I can estimate the height rise of the warm air from the adiabatic air charts which the weather department should have. Sherry will be here tomorrow, and she and I will work out the details. Tomorrow we will have enough information to specify the fans and exchangers. I hope you have enough cargo planes to pick up everything, pipe, heat exchangers and fans. Of course the ships have exchangers which could be relocated, but we will need many feet of pipe-. I estimate that it will take at least a week working night and day to get a few ships ready. Rome was not built in a day. We will need all the welders we can get. I suggest we start getting them as soon as possible. They should know what they are doing. We do not have time for leaks. Of course, we will test them briefly, but even one leak will hold us up." General Post says,

"I feel better already. Admiral Perry and John Harris, can we have the charts by 0800 tomorrow morning?"

"A chorus of yes answers."

"We will have the meeting start at 0800 (June 17) in the morning. Janice please hand each person a copy of the questions I proposed."

"I have the original and will have the copies in a few minutes."

"Thank you. The meeting is closed. See you tomorrow at 0800 AM. "Janice, let's go somewhere to relax, hold hands, look into those beautiful eyes and maybe have an early dinner."

"That would be nice, but I need to clean up and change clothes."

"Ok, don't take long, I need a drink."

CHAPTER 6

CHANGE IN PLANS AND NEWS FROM THE CLOUD

G ENERAL POST SAYS,

"Welcome to this early morning session. Janice and I had a relaxing evening and a wonderful dinner. I hope yours was also enjoyable. We have a lot of ground to cover this morning. The President will not be with us because he is busy and said this meeting would involve technical details. He shall get a summary. Before we start, we need progress reports. I just noticed we have new member, Cherry Jennings. You arrived last night, and I hope we made you comfortable."

"Yes, I had a good night and am looking forward to the task."

"We will get into that shortly. General Claassen, bring us up to date on the moon trip."

"The ship will arrive soon, but we have not had any word from them. According to NASA, who has been viewing them with the telescope, there does not seem to be any obvious problems. They appear to be preparing for a landing. The charts you requested are here. I suggest that we do a general review before we start studying for details." General Post says,

"Good Idea. May we hear from the Weather Dept.? John you are on."

"I have the wind charts and the adiabatic charts for several cities in the Southern Hemisphere."

"Thank you. It seems we have the information necessary to decide what to do. Patrick, fill us in on the probe. When is it to return, and have you been able to establish contact?"

"No we have not been able to contact the probe. Something has happened because the probe is no longer visible, and it should have been exiting The Cloud for the return trip. My guess is that the thing we have been unable to identify is a space ship. Since we got close to it for a picture, it may have some way of controlling the probe." General Post says,

"Another thing leading to Aliens. Do you have another probe we could send today which would stay far away from the thing? We need some data which may allow us to dissipate The Cloud."

"Yes, we always have a spare. I will call the office, and tell them to launch the second probe as soon as possible and to avoid the object."

"Patrick, you are always ahead of me. Can you make it do a faster job?"

"Yes I was planning on making a round trip in 10 hours. It is a lot of acceleration, but the equipment can stand it."

"Thank you, Patrick. You may go, but hurry back. Marilyn, have you heard any more about the seed and the animals which must survive?"

"Yes, the vendors know what to do about the seed, but they need to know the forecast of temperatures. You need to send the temperature-latitude chart to the Ag Dept., and they will see that the vendors receive it. Saving the animals, sheep, cows, chickens, ducks, horses (not used for food) and geese is more difficult because it involves many farmers and shipping of live animals. I recommend that we have a massive TV informational on the animals." Janice says,

"I will see that they get the chart and a letter of instructions." General Post says,

"Marilyn, you have another job. You have the information, and I think you should do the TV program. I have a suggestion. Show a few cities along with the latitude numbers since most people are not tuned to latitude. Also include a few cities in some of the countries in the Northern Hemisphere. They will also want to save the same food supply. Thanks for doing a bang up job. One other thing, how are the people in USA doing?" Marilyn,

"Things have calmed down. They seem to be confident that we are doing the best we can, and conditions have not worsened."

"I hate to run you off, but I think that TV show needs to be done soon. Thanks again. Well, ladies and gentlemen,

I think we are ready to view the charts. John, how is the Southern hemisphere divided?"

"They will show each continent with some ocean."

"Let us look at South America first." John Harris says,

"Every place on the east coast appears to have easterly component in the winds. The cities which we might affected are, Belem on the Amazon River, Recife, Rio de Janeiro, Montevideo and Buenos Aires. I have not included those places north of the equator. I think they may survive, but it will be quite cold for them. The west coast is hopeless. The winds are not from the west. Is that the way you all see it?"

"Yes. Ok, let's have a look at Africa." John Harris says,

"I think we can eliminate all north of 10 degrees N latitude which is just above the bottom of the bulge." General Post says,

"Is that ok with the rest of you. Raise your hand if you agree. Ok we are in agreement. John, how do the winds look along the west coast of Africa?"

"They do not look favorable and most of the cities are too far inland."

"Shall we temporarily leave them off the list? Raise your hands if you agree. I see we have agreement. The only other continents are New Zealand, Australia and a group of islands north of Australia. I don't think we can do much for the islands." "How does New Zealand look?" John Harris says,

"Auckland looks possible but the winds are not favorable for Wellington or Christ Church." General Post says,

"I would like to try to save them if we have enough nuclear ships. If you all agree, raise your hands. I see they are on the list. Let us look at Australia. John how does that look?"

"Australia has four cities which we ought to attempt to save. The winds are not perfect, but I think it will work. The cities are Adelaide, Brisbane, Sidney and Melbourne." General Post says,

"I like the Australians, I wish there was something more we could do for them. Their whole country is going to be an icebox even the most northern part. I will talk to the President and try to get him to talk to them. Tell them what we plan to attempt. Also ask them what they think. What else we might try? We have decided which cities we will try to help. Let us look at the ships available and figure which ones for each city and how many. Yes, Jeffery, I can see you have something to express." Jeffery Banks, presidential assistant, says,

"I have been sitting here thinking about how to mix the warm air across the wind flow direction. If you flew jet planes at low level back and forth across the wind wouldn't that mix the air? Also isn't the flow from the plane hot and moving at a high velocity. It seems that would do a better job of warming the city. What do you think?" There was cheer from the team. General Post says,

"That seems like a great idea, but flying at low levels may not be practical. That is something we must determine, but it would certainly add heat and mixing. It also means that only ships with aircraft could be used. Perhaps the other ships could supplement the Aircraft Carries. Admiral

Jason Perry, You did a lot of flying combat planes in your younger days. What do you think of the idea?"

"Hell, I wish I was young again; those young pilots always want to buzz something and show off for the girls. Maybe I will volunteer. No, this is going to be a tough job which only the young quickness can manage. You all realize that the process may form a cloud, and it may even rain over the city. I guess that a warm rain might be welcome. We will use a lot of aircraft fuel because we must fly at a slow speed for a jet plane, but I guess that will provide more energy. Perhaps the whole job could be done by airplanes and not require modifying the nuclear ships. The job could be started with in a few days. The only delay would be topping off the fuel tanks, and the time it takes for the ships to reach their destination. We know how much fuel they use per hour. That nuclear engineer can figure out how many airships would be needed for each place. Also the job would not be limited to the coastal places, but only limited by the number of planes we have. Perhaps Australia could do some of their town saving since they have three aircraft carries. This appears to be a task for the navy. They know about bombing missions, fuel consumption, planning, handling planes going and returning. This is just bombing missions. Turn us loose, we can do the job, and you can get on with removing The Cloud." General Post says,

"I like a volunteer, but this is more than a bombing mission. You will need to determine whether the mission is achieving the goal. If it is helping the area to be warmer or at least not frizzing to death, then we can expand to other areas." Admiral Peery says,

"I know what is required. We pride ourselves, that we know what we are doing. You have a tougher job, and I guess you won't know what you are doing until you succeed." General Post says,

"Yes, I guess you are right. Get the Navy going, and I will try to fix The Cloud. It is almost noon; let us have a quick lunch and get to work." Patrick jumps up and says,

"Not so fast. I just got a message in our code at the office. The engineers say they are receiving a message from the probe which they are recording. It seems that the probe has been captured by the spaceship. It will take a few minutes to decode and record on a disc."

"How soon will the disc be available?"

"We should hold lunch because they say that the message can be forwarded in about 15 minutes."

"Ok, Jeffery will you tell the kitchen to hold the lunch for 30 minutes."

"Yes, I will be back immediately; I can't miss the message. The President will want his own copy."

THE MESSAGE

We are aliens from another Planet with a similar Sun.

This message was coded because we have no time to communicate with the whole world, and we don't want to reveal our information. We are sending this message from your probe. We have wanted to communicate with the people on earth especially the United States, but our transmission system has been damaged. Your probe saved the day. We have also been saving power, and hope that we can get sufficient additional power to return home. We have been surveying your planet for 20000years, so we know quite bit about you. We look much like you and have visited your planet many times. We have not landed this time because we did not have enough power to make the landing. We are trapped, so to speak, in The Cloud. Our mission, this time, was to take over your planet after we adjusted the average temperature of the earth to about 10 degrees F. We were 95% sure that your survival numbers from the extreme cold of minus100 or more would be so small that you could not object. Our comfortable temperature is 10 degrees F which would be a struggle for you. We would control The Cloud to keep the temperature in our range. I guess you would like to know why we chose your planet. The biggest reason was that your sun will be stable for several billion years, and we could control the temperature to suit us. Also, we would use your infrastructure and not need to build it if we chose another planet. Our sun is about to go through the Red expansion stage which we can't control. Thus we would be burned to a crisp. Why are we talking to you? Our project has failed because the initial invasion force died from contact with you. We are confounded by this development because we have been frequently in contact during the past. We have stopped the invasion temporally until we can determine what killed our initial force. This will take several years because the analysis requires returning to our planet. None the less, we expect you to surrender.

We will leave The Cloud in place, but adjust so it won't be so severe until we return. We in this space ship have not contacted any one on the earth or from the earth. We disabled your units or killed them on the moon just before installing The Cloud. We noticed the ships which you sent. The failure of your radio communications was caused by The Cloud. We have restored the ability for you to communicate but will keep The Cloud heat screen in place. We believed that the cold you are experiencing will speed you to communicate. You must send someone who has the power to make decisions. We can use the power of your space ship to repair our transmission system. Don't be concerned with the power transmission. We have ways; your ship must be in contact with ours. You will be able to communicate with the moon, and you can communicate with us thru the probe. Come as soon as possible. We are signing off for now.

There was a stunned silence. General Claassen woke up first. "Well, I'll be dammed, we won a war without firing a shot. Post, it seems you are going to make a trip. What a development. I was about to give up." General Post says,

"Not so fast, we have not won yet. Yes, you may be right, but that decision is the President's. They have ask that we surrender; maybe we can negotiate. They need fuel, and we need them to turn that damned thing off before we freeze. Also they need their communications fixed. Marilyn. I see you have returned. You could not have gotten that TV show about saving animals done so quickly. What is the schedule of the TV show?"

"I hired a writer who is great getting peoples' attention. I figured that this show required more exciting format, than I was capable of producing. He will have it done tomorrow, and I can review it in the afternoon. If it is ok, he will get it recorded with actors tomorrow night, and I can review it during the morning of the 19th. I expect to broadcast that same evening during prime time. We will show it several times a day on several channels to be sure it reaches everyone who needs it."

"Thank you, Marilyn; did you hear the message from the space ship in The Cloud?"

"Yes, would you like for me to get the President?

"Yes, while we discuss continuing the Southern Hemisphere project." Admiral Jason Perry,

"I think it is too early to abandon it because we don't know what those bastards in The Cloud are going to do as yet." General Claassen says,

"I agree, I think we should charge ahead until you have some agreement we can accept. That Cloud may not be as easy to foil as indicated by the message." General Post says,

"So we continue the heating of the Southern Hemisphere as agreed. Raise your hand, if you agree. Admiral you are free to continue until further notice, and Marilyn the TV show shall also continue. Harold Wilson and Cherry Jennings, You should continue with the conversions which we discussed before the airplane idea was suggested. We may need both methods to keep our southern friends from freezing." They answered in a chorus of yes. Harold and Cherry comment,

"We have discussed the subject and know what to do. We are planning on calling some venders for fans and heat exchangers tomorrow. We will need at least two cargo ships. This job will take at least two weeks to complete. We will discuss with the Admiral which ships he will allow us to convert. Also the Navy has several welders which they can supply. We are ready to go." General Post says,

"I am not sure that will be soon enough; they might be well frozen by then, but continue I think General Claassen can supply the cargo ships. I see that Marilyn has returned with the President. Mr. President, we have heard from the object in The Cloud which has been identified as a space ship. Play the disc again for the President." The disc takes a few minutes to play." When it is completed, the President says.

"It is obvious that we must deal with them. We might survive on our own initiative, but they have all the cards. It is my job, but I would not survive the takeoff and landing. This has to be a person who can represent me and is in shape to survive the trip. There is only one man who could survive and knows me well enough to manage the job. General Post you have been nominated." Janice jumps up,

"What am I to do? Where does that leave me? I can't give up a husband. I know what these space trips can do!!"

"Honey don't get excited; we don't know any details. I told you I would work out an acceptable plan."

"I am ready to have children, and I don't want you gallivanting all over the universe."

"What if you go along? You are very good at negotiating and better than I. I need to make this trip; without doing it, we won't need or have time for children. I think we can make a deal which will give us survival. They may attack again in the future. For them to make a round trip to their Planet, it should require several years, and give us time to be ready when they return. I will try to get them to leave and give us The Cloud control, and you will be a great help. Please make the trip with me. We will have at least a day to discuss our future."

"Well ok, I hope you settle down and just teach at the college. Maybe you can write your memories, and I can be scared again reading them." The President says,

"Well, I guess that is settled. Are you sure you are physically able to make such a trip? You will need to be checked to make sure you are not already pregnant. I don't think we could allow you to go if you were. How soon can you get this project launched?" Patrick says,

"The ship can be ready on the 19th and can be launched at that time if General Post and Janice are ready." General Post says,

"Since neither one of us is familiar with the operation of a space ship, we want two persons who do understand the controls; two more who can fix whatever breaks and a bunch of spare parts per the fixers. I only want to make this trip once. Also, have two other ships ready to bring whatever parts our guests may request. I want to make sure they survive, leave here, and tell us how to deal with The Cloud. I suspect that they will want some nuclear power materials and food." Patrick says,

"Whatever they request, we will move fast to see that they get it. The two spare ships are ready but will take a day or two to launch depending on what you learn" The President says,

"From what I see and have read, this group has covered the possibilities of combating the cold weather. You and Janice ought to go. You have much to do if the launch is to stay on schedule. I am appointing Marilyn to chair the group which will meet at 9 AM every day to review project status and make changes if necessary. She will also have the responsibility to keep the world and I informed. Marilyn, it is your meeting." General Post says,

Not so fast, I think we can get them to turn down The Cloud if that is possible, at least temporally while we have a discussion. The President should send them a message through our probe, that General Post will be coming and will represent the President. Janice and I are departing. It is all yours Marilyn, wish us luck.

"I will take the job of informing the world. I think we can adjourn. See you all tomorrow at 9 AM.

CHAPTER 7

A FEW PRIVATE THOUGHTS

LATE AFTERNOON JUNE 17, 2111

ARON AND JANICE, HE SAYS,
"What a day, you and I will have a busy day tomorrow getting ready for our trip. Perhaps we should have a relaxing time and go to bed early to night."

"No, I feel like we should have a fling. We can rest tomorrow night. I would like to go dancing, have a nice dinner, go home early, take a shower with you rubbing my back, and then we can stay naked for the rest of the night. What do you think about that, and what do you think the two love birds, Harold and Cherry, will do? I bet they won't be relaxing."

"You are probably right, and also you're a little crazy, but I feel up to a crazy evening. I think before I forget it; I must call Patrick while you get dressed for our night on the town." *He needs to tells Patrick to send a message to the space ship, that we will leave here on the 19th and probably get to their space ship early the 20th or maybe late the 19th.*

"Ok, I will be just a minute. I will put on the blue dress which did not change color." *He talks to Patrick for a few minutes.* Harold Wilson and Cherry Jennings, He says,

"Cherry, let's have an evening on the town. Do you know where you can dance the old way cheek to cheek and get a good dinner?"

"No, I have never stayed in Washington, but I would enjoy your suggestion. Tomorrow is going to be a tough day. You don't suppose that General knows a place. He is a rough looking all business guy, but I bet he knows all the places. He has that beautiful wife, and he didn't get her being all business. They seem to love each other. Harold! Give him a shout before he gets into that apartment."

"Hey! Wait a second" The General turns and says,

"What?"

"We have a question." They approach.

"Can you recommend a place which has old time cheek to cheek dance music and a decent dinner? Cherry and I want to have a good time before the work descends tomorrow."

"That is where we are going. Why don't you come with us; it is not far, but we will need to take a taxi. If you need to freshen up, meet us in this hallway in about 15 minutes. I think my wife will enjoy the company."

"Great, we will meet you here in a few." The two couples went to Fareenes, a new private club run by an Italian who was a nut about old dance music. It was a great dinner; there was lots of hand holding and dancing. It was great fun, and they changed partners some. Harold ask a few questions about the trip to The Cloud for which the General did not give much information. Janice was a little looser, but she had no idea what her husband thought because he did not say anything. He was unaccountably silent which surprised her, but she did not say anything. When they got back to their apartment, she ask him,

"What was going on?" He said,

"Ask me tomorrow; I don't want to talk about anything; I want a secret meeting with you. Are you ready for that shower?"

"Yes, let's go. I bet I can get my clothes off first."

General Claassen's wife says,

"What do you look so cheerful about? Since this cloud thing, you have been dragging in every evening as if you had lost you best friend or that mangy old dog. By the way where is the dog?"

"Oh, I dropped him off for a bath at the kennel this morning. Well, The Cloud thing may be solved. Today we heard from that thing in The Cloud; it turned out to be a space ship from another star. Their mission, which was to wipe us out, failed because the initial invasion group died except for the ones in the space ship. They have said they must return home but will leave The Cloud in place. We look like winners, but they said we were to surrender. I have never had a war in which we won without a shot. Why would I not be cheerful? It seems that the General Post and his wife will be going to the space ship in The Cloud on the 19th to negotiate a better deal. I hope they are successful since firing a shot might get more problems.

I am glad it is them and not me. Of course, if he pulls it off, he will be the hero and his wife too. Oh by the way, Generals don't drag themselves in."

"You remember that girl who has been doing some house work. Well, she has prepared a special dinner for us tonight. I told her what our favorite dishes were, and she said we would enjoy what she prepared. So we can both relax beside the fireplace, and enjoy the heat it supplies on this cold June day while we wait for dinner."

"Have I got time to get the dog?

"Yes, hurry up. The supper won't be ready until 6."

"Oh something else is to happen. You know I told you about the Gulf Stream project. That has been dropped for another goofy idea to save some areas in the Southern Hemisphere which will get much colder, at least 100 degrees below 0. This one is to use jet planes to form a heated cloud over a large area with the hot planes exhaust. Admiral Perry thinks it might work. He feels it might keep them from freezing."

"Sometimes crazy ideas work. Hurry up and get your dog."

John Belltone, USA President) and his wife, Marion.

"John, I see you are a little tired this evening. Dinner won't be ready until 7. Let us sit by the fireplace, and you can tell me about your day."

"Good idea. I have been President for almost 6 years, and I promised more that I could chew."

"Well you have done a lot. Through your efforts you have seen the size of the government reduced and managed to limit congressional terms. Here it is a 100years later than the march toward socialism when we have returned to democracy." The American people rejected socialism which proves they understood the peril.

"That is true, but with real power I could have accomplished much more. I think perhaps The Cloud will give us all the power to do anything I think necessary. Who can fight if they are freezing? We heard from a space ship in The Cloud which has reduced worldwide temperatures. Their mission was to take over our planet because their sun was dying and would burn their planet to a cinder. The two in the space ship are the only survivors of the first settlers. Apparently they died from a strange disease when they met our people on the moon. One of the things they offered on the second message was for us to keep The Cloud, and give us the method to control temperatures from 0 up to our desires. I think they also meant that individual sections could be controlled. That means we could keep rogue nations from getting out of control without firing a shot or blowing them up."

"I don't think that is a good solution. What happens if the control data is stolen? You know how difficult it was to keep a secret. I think we should destroy The Cloud and the control data. Why let another Genie escape? Did we learn anything with the atom? This one we could destroy; no one would be wiser, and no one could develop it without help of our visitors."

"Once it has been demonstrated, someone in the world will work on developing something similar and we might as well have the knowledge. Well, it is just a piece of equipment which we can be used for good or bad. You know that we would use it for good except in special cases. Even if the secret got out, we probably could override any bad effects. I guess it would be a war of cloud control which might end in a tie, and we would then need to talk."

"I don't like it. In a hundred or a thousand years who knows what will happen. Once The Cloud is here, someone might be able to negate your controls, and the war would be over. Perhaps we would be the losers. You better think about this long and hard before you accept such a weapon. I don't think anyone could develop it from scratch."

"I will consider it because I value your opinion. I will have a couple of days before General Post flies. I may just take two days of vacation for contemplation. General Post and his wife are going to the space ship in The Cloud to negotiate terms. I need to find an appropriate title for him since he will be representing me. The beings in the space ship will expect him to have complete authority to deal."

CHAPTER 8

GENERAL CLAASSEN: WE ARE STILL AT WAR!

9 AM MEETING JUNE18 2111

*T*HE PERSON IN CHARGE IS *Marilyn Linden, who has taken General Post's place. She has brought her secretary, Sandra Field, to replace Janice.*

Present for The Cloud Meeting: General Mike Claassen, Admirable Jason Perry, Harold Wilson, Cherry Jennings, John Harris, Patrick Bartell, John Rison, Jan Pearson, Frank Harrison, Charles Massey, Jeffery Banks and President Belltone. Marilyn says,

"As you know General Post and Janice are on their way to Cape Canaveral for the flight to the space ship in The Cloud. The President interrupts,

"I need to talk to Post before he departs. He can be back here in less than a hour if he has not landed that plane. Claassen get him on the radio and tell him to get back as soon as possible. I guess you will need to find out where he is if he is not in the plane. He is to return if the space ship has not been launched. We have news he needs to know and discuss. The launch is tomorrow so there is plenty of time. That plane he is using is very fast." General Claassen calls on his phone and radio, but the General does not answer. He calls all morning on both the phone and airplane communications. He finally at 1 o'clock catches him in the plane which was fortunate because Post was starting to pull out the microphone plugs and turning off commutations temporally to talk to Janice.

"The President orders you to return to Washington post haste. We have new information which you need to discuss with the President."

"Why don't we use that fancy TV in the President's office which allows one to see and talk to the other person or a group in real time? My wife thinks it is great for buying dresses or other clothing."

"Claassen give me the mike." Almost jerking it from his hand, he shouts,

"Get your ass BACK up here. When General Post arrives, tell him to come to my office, immediately."

"Yes Sir." Marilyn says,

"I can tell you that the TV show for informing the world how to save the animals will be shown tonight on several stations. I reviewed it this morning, and got the time scheduled with the TV stations. General Claassen, Let us have an update on the moon trip."

"We have finally heard from them. They found many dead in all three units, and the power was turned off. We restarted the power. In a few hours some Americans,

Chinese and Russians came out of the mines where they were able to survive. It was fortunate that we arrived when we did because they could not have survived much longer. There were many more bodies than were stationed on the moon. When we actually started looking, we found the aliens were the ones in tight fitting suits made of some very tough materials. They also had a breathing helmet. We know what to do with our dead. What do you want us to do with the dead Aliens? Of course, it was quite cold when we arrived, but it is warming up inside. There are some aliens in space suits inside and outside. We have no idea what the inside warm or outside cold will do the dead alien's bodies. Since they turned off the power, they must like the cold, so we put the inside bodies outside. I told the troops to do nothing with the aliens until we heard from General Claassen. What shall I tell them?" President Belltone says,

"Tell them to keep all the aliens in cold storage at normal atmospheric pressures. We don't know what extremes will do to them, and the aliens in the space ship may have their own disposal plan. We would like to know what killed them. If you can get blood samples, do so and send to us as soon as possible. Keep the blood samples refrigerated." General Glaassen,

Sandra, I think you can send that message directly from your machine. I changed my mind; for security, we will send by LBT, Light Beam Transfer which limits detection. I am sending on the 20th a larger group who are trained for moon duty. The first personnel will stay and help the new unit to clean up and get the equipment running. I will inform the Russians and the Chinese about their losses. I suppose both will blame us and expect a little bowing and scraping. Mr. President, I think it would be better for you to contact them. I would rather not take responsibility for foreign affairs." Marilyn says,

"Thank you General. Admiral Perry, Where are we on the warming up some of the Southern Hemisphere?"

"I have sent an aircraft carrier fully loaded with aircraft and fuel to Panama because it is much closer and also colder. The ship is quite fast and should arrive in about 50 hours. It could do a quick test to demonstrate feasibility of heating with a warm cloud. I also started a ship with aircraft on its way to Argentina to get a head start. We already have temperature devices which can send a radio signal from several places in Panama. Also, it will take one or two days to get more ships ready with fuel. As each ship is ready, it will depart. The temperature devices which can be dropped and tested will be delivered to each ship by air, and dropped before the heating flights are done." Jeffery says,

"if you are going to drop them from a plane, why not fly directly from USA. It would be quicker to drop and test long before the aircraft carriers could get there." Admiral Perry says,

"I thought of that, and discarded the idea because our pilots are trained on weather instruments, and we can know the temperatures several hours before we are ready to launch the heating project. We will know the results of the Panama venture before the rest of the carriers reach their destinations in South America or Africa." Marilyn says,

"If the group agrees, you can go ahead. If you agree, hold up your right hand. We have agreement. Admiral it appears you have the project under control. We will want to know the results as soon as you know. Harold and Sherry, what is the status of ship modifications to heat the air with heat exchangers and fans?"

"We have calculated the size of fans and heat exchangers. General Claassen has agreed to supply the cargo planes, as soon as we can tell him the pickup place. Admiral Perry will have the welders here a day before the materials arrives. He has also specified which ships are to be converted. To shorten the time of delivery, we will call the vendors to assess what is available in the range we think is needed without waiting for fabrication. We hope to have at least one ship ready within one week for a test run. We think Panama would be the place for the test. We will pick a ship which can pass thru the canal. We expect to test outside the canal and within the canal to determine the best solution. We have suggested that we also do a combined test with the jets and air heating with fans. Admiral Perry promised he would have an aircraft carrier available in that time frame." Marilyn says,

"General Claassen, I think you have something to say."

"I know you did not hear the message from the moon since the volume was turned down. The Captain says that they are unable to get a blood sample because the needle will not penetrate the alien suit. We have tried cutting and drilling without any luck. The suit is soft and pliable but is tough beyond belief. We tried to remove a suit but were unsuccessful. Some of these aliens seem not to be dead but to be in a suspended animation state. What if they wake up? They are scary! We have not seen anything that they used for a weapon, but they killed a bunch of the units' personnel. There are some dead Americans, Russians and Chinese in undamaged space suits, and yet they died with their oxygen still flowing. We are tempted to load Aliens on a space ship, and fire it off into the sun, but we will wait to be told what to do." General Claassen says,

"Well, The Cloud Committee has a situation in which no one of us has any experience. I dislike waiting, but our only source of information will be General Post, and his negotiations with the Aliens in The Cloud." Marilyn says,

"Does anyone else want to make a suggestion?" Charles Massey says,

"I suggest that we inform General Post and the President who left a few minutes before this revelation. Furthermore tell those soldiers to put the Aliens in a space ship and seal the doors so they can only be opened from the outside. I believe the live Aliens will want to decide the fate of the moon Aliens. If we don't give them a choice, they may take some unpleasant action."

"If you agree with General Claassen and Charles' suggestion raise your right hand. Ok, it is agreed that we will contact General Post and the President with the information and proposed action. The President will decide if he agrees with the action." John Harris says,

"While we are waiting, I would like to say a few words about The Cloud. If we keep The Cloud and controls as indicated by the aliens, we will have constraint problems with nations wanting us to adjust their temperature. It is impossible to say what changes will occur when the natural state is artificially changed. If we plan to use it as a weapon to gain certain objectives, the result in weather or national relations may not be to our advantage. The Weather Bureau is already seeing changes which indicate that storm severity will be substantially increased. I think, even if we get rid of The Cloud, we will see changes which will last for several years before it reaches the stability we enjoyed before The Cloud arrived. Messing with nature before we know what we are doing can lead to unpleasant results. Weather is bad enough now; what happens if we get 6 hurricanes or 6 tornadoes or worse? Are you ready for worldwide catastrophes? This committee's job is just beginning." The President had returned and says,

"Don't be so dramatic, John. The world is a tough place. Do you really believe the weather can get too bad?"

"It has happened in the past when 90 % of the animals perished. I think we should make plans, and if it does not happen, then I will be happy to be wrong." President says,

"I want to keep The Cloud for a couple of reasons. First it is a weapon, and secondly if we ever have global warming, we can correct for it with The Cloud. I don't plan to use it as a weapon, but you never know what may happen, and we might need to use it." Charles Massey,

"Can you keep someone else from using it? You are only going to be President for another two years. How are we going to keep this genie in the box? There are many who would use it if they got the controls. We were not able to keep the Atom bomb in the box; what makes you think we can today or in the future, a thousand years from now? You have some of the best minds here in The Cloud Committee. And, I think, the Committee should debate the problem which I have stated." The President says,

"Ok, we will do that, but in the meantime, we will keep The Cloud and adjust it to return to the normal sun radiation. We will keep the Cloud Committee, and when General Post returns from his mission, the group will reconvene. Can you accept this for the time being?"

"If that is the best I can get, it is OK."

"The members of The Cloud Committee will continue these meetings until General Post returns from negotiating with the Aliens. When General Post and Janice get here, send both to my office."

General Claassen says,

"Listen everybody, there is a message coming from General Post."

"We are on final approach to Dulles Airport. Send the helicopter, and we can miss the ground traffic."

"Ok, it will be on its way shortly. When you get here, you and Janice go directly to the President's office."

"Thanks, he is a little hot today. Do I need to be subservient? See you later."

"Maybe?" General Claassen says,

"Listen there is another message from the moon."

"This is the Captain. Just as were finishing up loading the Aliens in a rocket ship, one of them woke up and killed one of my men without touching him, how weird. We shot him several times, but I think we just knocked him unconscious. We loaded him and locked the door shut. Then we fired the rocket in an orbit around the moon. From the orbit, we can send it anywhere in the universe when we get the order. I am not sure what the Aliens can do from orbit, and I hope we get an order soon." General Claassen says,

"Sandra, send this information to the President's office. He will need it when General Post arrives. I should have known that this battle was too easy. The Aliens had us out flanked and may still. I need to talk to General Post before he leaves. Send another message to the President's office telling Post to see me before he leaves for the Cape."

The President's Office:

"General Post, I think you were trying to avoid me, and therefore have a freer hand. You left so quickly last night and this morning, that I did not have time to give you instructions. Also, several things have happen on the moon which might affect the negotiating process. So it is good; that you did not get away. I want to keep The Cloud and the controls for keeping reckless nations in line, and just in case global warming becomes a problem."

"What I see, is that The Cloud may cause bigger problems with the nations, and as for global warming the scientific view is that the world appears to be getting colder. Also, the Aliens may return especially if we keep The Cloud which they could control over our methods. They apparently need it to occupy our earth at some colder temperature"

"I think we can protect ourselves adequately. We need this equipment to move the world toward a more global government with little power and to outlaw war. War is destructive and wastes resources which could be better used. I happen to be one who does not believe a bigger stronger government is best for the people. The bigger the government the more dictatorial they become. They move away from what the people need toward what the government needs."

"Well I work for you, and you are the boss. I will do what you want."

"On your way out, go see what Claassen wants. Have a safe trip; I will be looking forward to seeing you when you get back." In the hallway he whispers to Janice,

"See what I mean. He has lost his mind and judgment."

"Shush, the walls have ears." They arrive at the conference room. General Claassen says,

"Am I glad to see you! Close the door. Did the President tell you about what is happening on the moon?"

"No, he was busy telling me what he wanted and why." General Claassen hands a copy of the Moon Message and says,

"We are up against a civilization far more advanced than ours. I think, they can do whatever they want to do. They have been watching us for 20,000 years. Be careful when you negotiate with them. They may have other goals, than the ones they stated. For instance how do they know that their comrades were killed when they were not? What are we to believe or not?"

"Thanks for the information. It only bolsters my feelings of dread. The President may be walking in to a trap. I will try to do what he wants, but it will be difficult. Janice and I hope this trip ends happily for us." General Claassen says,

"Oh, something else you need to know. The President has agreed to have the Cloud Committee discuss and recommend disposition of The Cloud after you return from space."

"Thanks again, we are off to the helicopter and The Cloud."

FLYING TO CAPE CANAVERAL

It is June 18 in the mid-afternoon, General Post and Janice are in a private airplane, so he and his wife can have a private conversation, while they are flying to Cape Canaveral for the trip to The Cloud. They rented the plane because he wanted to talk about The Cloud, and he did not want any word to get out. All microphones were unplugged and incoming message turned off. Aaron spoke to Janice,

"I want you to know that I love you, and I would do almost anything you might want, but I have a dilemma. Let me explain before you start the question session. I think I know the President better than he knows himself. I knew him before he was President when he ran a large corporation. I feel that he loves power although he has not shown it as President. Even some of the conversations we have had during his term, have revealed his desire for power. He, I think, will use The Cloud to gain other objectives, such as forcing peace on some countries. I am under the impression that The Cloud can be controlled in sections, so that only one area could feel the cold. It seems to me that the area would need to be quite large for a particular area to feel very cold temperatures locally. This means those countries outside the one being punished would also be punished. That would not be fair, and the mistreated countries would complain. Perhaps they would start a shooting war. Today almost anyone could bomb USA, but they are afraid we would retaliate. Suppose that someone steals the controls or we get some President who has fewer scruples. This kept me awake last night for several hours. Well, I decided that I must not let the genie escape if you agree. As you know I have received his instructions. I plan to destroy The Cloud and the controls. But it will seem like treason. Think of what we might be accused. I am not sure what you would get, but I would be tried for treason and probably shot. Let me tell you about the escape I have planned. This plane is not a rental; I bought it for 20 million dollars."

"You! What! Where did you get 20 million dollars?"

"Honey, there is a lot you don't know about me, and if we have time, you will get the full story. I think my days working for the government are over, however this comes out. We are worth considerably more. I don't know just how much, but it is at least 300 million, and that is just cash. I have it spread around in several places under different names. I have been planning to disappear for several years if it became necessary. You take this airplane; it can fly at 150000 ft. at 10,000 mph and can go nonstop to any place in the world. I have friends all over the world that could hide you and ne for a price of course, or we can change our names. I would rather stay in Colorado and continue teaching in college while we have those children. I never told you because you might have said something which could have compromised my position, and beside that I did not want you to worry unnecessarily. Well, you are sitting there with your mouth open. What do you say?"

"Ah, ah, I don't know. What do I say when a husband turns into a stranger? Why have we not used some of that money?"

"We have. Any time you wanted something, there was always money for it, and you never ask from where it came."

"I think I would like go home and forget all of this, but I can't because we are going to save the world. That reminds me. You said you were going to destroy The Cloud, and you were going to be shot. I suggest that you give the President what he wants. I think it will prove to be a false weapon because the only way it really works is when it affects the whole world. You said yourself that it would only be effective for a single country if a large area around that country was affected. The innocent surrounding area would protest or start a real war. I think the President will abandon it for normal procedures. Let him decide, and we can go home and kiss the government goodbye."

"The problem I have with that is that some rogue government could steal the controls and freeze the world but protect themselves long enough to win."

"Yes, but as soon as the President realizes that The Cloud does not work efficiently on small areas, you can persuade him to destroy The Cloud. No one could develop a new Cloud without the alien's help even if they had the controls. Then we are free without the treason thing hanging over us. Perhaps you can get him to do it while we are on this trip before it can ever be used. It is better to be hero than a scoundrel."

"OK honey, we will try it your way, but I am not talking to the President until I have all the facts. I am not sure I know how to destroy The Cloud completely. In the meantime, I will have the plane refueled and prepared for a long trip just in case we need it. I have planned in the past, and a few times it saved my ass."

"I thought those secret trips you took were more dangerous than your nonchalant attitude indicated. You did not want me to worry, but I did anyway. Ending this government attachment will be a happy day. You don't have any more secrets do you; I hope not?"

Well no, nothing that matters. It was something I enjoyed, and I will be sorry to leave, but the time has come to do other things." *Although he can hear voice communications, he can't reply, so he plugs in the microphones as they approach the air field. They land; General Post tells them to refuel, check the plane for malfunctions and have ready to fly in two days fully loaded.*

General Claassen says,

"Fortunately Jeffery was not present to hear this conversation, and I hope the rest of you can keep your mouths closed. General Post has a tough job to do, and there is no one else who can do justice for all of us. Here comes another message from the moon."

"This is the Captain again. We have had one of the Aliens come out of the mines. He surrendered and seems friendly. He had an insigne on his uniform, whereas the others did not which indicates that he is some kind of an official. What are we to do with him or her? Oh yes, he speaks perfect English. The heat drove him out of the mine. We have a room which is much cooler, so he is in there." Marilyn replies,

"We will discuss it and let you know. What a day, we have dead ones; one who rises up and kills a solder, then we have one who comes out of hiding when it gets too hot; he speaks English fluently and is friendly. What do we do now, anybody?" Admiral Perry says,

"I suggest, we try to get some information from him. Perhaps we can compare it with what General Post gets. I think we should help the Captain by providing him with some questions." Marilyn says,

"Jeffery you just got back. Did you hear that the solders had captured an Alien?"

"Yes I did. The initial questions should be ones to which we know the answers. Maybe when we get in to ones we don't know, he won't realize we are ignorant and will give true answers. Let us get them down, and then we can arrange them in order or eliminate some. My first question is: how long have you considered moving your civilization to the earth? And no 2, what do we call your star?" Marilyn says,

"Anyone else?" Charles Massey says,

"I do. Why are you so friendly and cooperative?" Harold and Jeffery also suggested questions.

Marilyn says.

"I think maybe we have enough questions for now. Perhaps a subcommittee of Charles Massey and General Claassen will arrange them in order for The Cloud Committee to review. If we want to give the results to General Post, we must get these to the Captain early this afternoon. Will you Charles and General agree to do this immediately?"

"Yes." *The rest of the Cloud Committee leaves to check on their various jobs, while Charles and Claassen gather around Sandra and the computer. She does the arranging as they tell her the order. The list is ready to send.* Patrick says,

"Yes, we can specify that we use the LTB going and returning. We want to be sure that none of this gets to the space ship in The Cloud. Maybe General Post can find out what they know. You know the moon transmissions were by radio. We need to make sure all communications are by LTB. I thought of this before and equipped General Post's ship with the LTB."

CHAPTER 9

SECETS, PARANOIA, TRUST

JUNE18 2111 8 PM MEETING

THE MEETING HAS RECONVENED AT 8 PM to review the answered questions. The Captain reported,

The Alien was very cooperative, and said he loved America, and he was not happy with the invasion. He had lived in United States since the Revolution of 1776. It was because he demanded that the invasion should be done in the summer to permit the Americans to survive. He volunteered that he loved America so much that he wanted to have children, but all three wives he had miscarried within a month after they became pregnant. He loved his wives and was most unhappy with his sexual incompatibility. The next answer you need is how old is this man. He said 5000 years in our time frame. Also he said they normally lived 10,000years. He said that he had much more to tell us, but he wanted to answer the questions first. The following are the questions and answers.

The Corrected List of Questions

1. How long have you considered moving your civilization to the earth? 2000 years and we could have waited another 5000years. Our sun will go through the red expansion in 10,000 years and burn us up.

2. What do we call your star? I don't know. It is 62 light years from your sun.

3. How long did it take your ship to reach our star? 68.2light years which is 90% of light speed. That is impossible with your technology.

4. How long would it take with our technology to reach your star? I guess it would take several million years.

5. How did you kill our solders? We have a mental attack on their brain which causes a stroke. We must be very close to the subject. We have other weapons which they will probably use during the next attempt as well as The Cloud.

6. Why did you surrender? I want to stay in America. Of the worlds you have the best society which results from your freedom.

7. Why are you so friendly and cooperative? I just told you.

8. Is The Cloud a permanent thing? Yes it can be destroyed but with great difficulty. You are stuck with it, but they may give you the control.

9. Does The Cloud gradually dissipate? Well Yes, its half-life is 10000 years or so.

10. If so, do you know how you would regenerate it? We know how if it has not completely dissipated.
11. What average temperature would you have set for your people? 20 degrees Fahrenheit
12. What caused your people to die? We are very sensitive to strong electromagnetic energy. That is why we wear these suits, but even that can be over whelmed. Some die but others are unconscious for a while. I do not know where the energy was generated.
13. Where do you think your comrades are now? Well, I have seen a ship circling the moon. I suppose they are in it.
14. Did you know that two or more of your citizens are surviving in a space ship trapped in The Cloud and have ask for our help to return to your planet? No. They will want to take their people in the ship back home with them. They will use the ship in which they came. You should help them to return if they will agree to give you The Cloud control. Otherwise they could get very nasty. They could make the world a big ball of ice. They will wonder what happen to me so don't tell them.
15. Mars is vacant, and you could have supplied oxygen, and it does have water; why did you select the earth instead of Mars? No infrastructure and not enough water or metals. We did not want the job of construction or mining.
16. Although you failed this time, are there plans to try again? Yes they will preplan, but it will be a few

hundred years. I will get you ready to stop their attack.

17. You have the ability to move around in the universe; were there any other planets which might have been acceptable, and why did you chose the earth? No. There are a number of planets but no infrastructures.

18. Have you been on the earth before, and how long did you stay? Yes I was here 4000 years ago and left after a short time. Returned during your Revolution, and I stayed until now.

19. How long have you been observing us, and did you help some of the earth people? 20000years but did not help anyone.

Marilyn says,

"Patrick, are you sure you can send this information by LTB to a moving ship?"

"Yes, the ship must not be accelerating and is moving close to an inline path. The beam must be locked on before we can transmit. Once the beam is locked on, the ship can move around, and the beam will stay locked. The transmission is completed in few seconds. You realize that they are in Cape Canaveral until early tomorrow. For security we will still use the LTB. To get his attention I have a coded radio message which no one will understand except him. When he is ready, he will return the message, and then we will hook up and send the LTB message. I will call NASA now to get ready. This message is already in their computer, so this paper copy we can keep for our records. They have already sent the radio message, and we are waiting for the reply. They will call me when the LTB message has been sent and the General's reply. We will be able to hear the negotiating which will not begin until late on 19th or early the 20th," Marilyn says,

"Is there any further business to discuss?" Admiral Perry says,

"We will start the test on Panama tomorrow morning. That is all I have." Harold says,

"The stuff we ordered for the first ship conversion should arrive tomorrow after noon. The rest are scheduled to arrive in 4 to 5 days. The welders should also arrive tomorrow." General Claassen says,

"The replacement crews for the moon will fly late tomorrow. I have sent a LTB message to the moon to return the alien to earth with the temporary workers. We will keep him under wraps with the special military unit until the situation clarifies. We will ask him to remove his protective suit before he leaves the moon. If any one sees him, they will think he is just one of our soldiers." John Harris says,

"I think the President should tell the people where we stand on this Cloud project, leaving out that we have captured an alien. I think we should keep that a state secret for now because we do not want the Aliens to know. What we tell the people will give them confidence, that we are making progress. Then tell them that there is a terrible winter storm brewing in northern Canada and Alaska. It is only a few days from descending upon us. I think it has developed to the point that no matter what we do about The Cloud; it will still hit." Marilyn says,

"Sandra, print a memo covering these two items, and I will take it to the President. Are there any other items? Patrick says,

"I have just heard from NASA. General Post has received the information in Cape Canaveral, and he believes it will be a great help in negotiating."

"Good, there seems little more we can do tonight. Let us adjourn and meet again tomorrow at 9 AM." Admiral Perry,

"I suggest we meet tomorrow afternoon, say 2 PM. There won't be much to report early, and we may start hearing from General Post later in the meeting." Marilyn says,

"Is that agreeable to the committee."

"Yes, change the time to 2PM."

MEETING 2 PM, JUNE 19, 2110

Marilyn says,

"I see everyone is present. Admiral Perry, how is the experiment going."

"It has been a great success. There is a gentle warm rain falling over Panama. We raised the temperature about 60 degrees, and I think we could have increase it even more. We had to use 2 airplanes all the time. There was not complete coverage all the time which we could eliminate with more planes, and thus raise the temperature in colder places. There was some concern about too much hydrocarbon being exhausted, but we dropped detectors.

The fuel burn was more complete than expected because the detectors showed no hydrocarbons on the ground. The ship has been dispatched to the Belem area. It will take 50 hours to make the 3000 miles trip. The rest of the Air Craft Carriers are their way to other needy places. With our success, I am reneging on my promise to do a combined test with Harold's and Cherry's project. They will just fly on their own." Marilyn says,

"That is great news. Harold, what is the status of your project?"

"We were on the ship early this morning and got the welders started. They should be finished by now, and we will leave soon to inspect the job. If it is ok, the ship will leave immediately for Panama."

"John, is there anything more on the storm?"

"It now appears that the storm will start in 2 to 4 days. It is much larger than we have ever seen. The temperature will be 20 or 30 below zero, and the winds over a 100 mph. We are forecasting it to hit USA in 3 to 4 days. It will be very disruptive to business and the people. We expect two foot of snow in the northern areas and a foot or less in the southern part of USA. I think that the President should get on TV and tell the people to be sure to have enough clothing and food for two weeks. His message should be recorded and repeated frequently. Also keep all children and animals inside especially when the winds start. A 75 mph will cause damage and pick up a person."

"Well John, I hope you are wrong; we don't need any more problems. General Claassen do you have any more news?"

"The moon trained personnel were shipped this morning. The Alien reported, that he must keep the suit on for protection until he lands on the earth. We will need to make sure there are no reporters or other blabber mouths anywhere near when he arrives. Make sure he is in a safe room and has a guard."

"General, I am sure you can take care of that problem. Patrick, have we heard from General Post."

"No, we probably won't until 8 PM, and I don't think we will hear much because it is so late."

"My animal TV show has limited movement of them unless they are kept from freezing. Since there is no further business, let us break-up until 8 PM." They all leave. It was no surprise that Harold and Sherry left together, but Marilyn and the weather man left together after he ask her to dine with him.

8 PM MEETING JUNE 19, 2110

The meeting had reconvened, and Marilyn had turned up the sound so everybody could hear the negotiations. She also turned on the recorder for a record. General Post had said. they would start in 60 seconds. General Post and Janice had arrived at the ship in The Cloud and were maneuvering to make a gentle contact with ship. General Post gave up and told Janice that she had the gentle touch, and perhaps she could make the contact without making a mess. After several tries the contact was made. General Post said,

"I am certainly glad you came along; you did a great job. After the greetings, you can handle the negotiating."

"Are you abdicating a tough job?"

"NO! I am bowing to the superior women's intuition."

"This is General Aaron Post sent here by The President of United States to negotiate a peace between your government and the world." The Alien said,

"You must wait a few moments while we use your power to repair our system. We are satisfied, that you came. We have watched your career in ways that you can't imagine and know you have the President's ear. We know that you are a man of your word. Before we start, we want to know the purpose of the beam of light between the earth and the moon."

"We did not think you could see it because the beam is so faint. Information which we did not want to share before this meeting was transmitted through the light beam."

"We did not see it; we detected it. We have finished our repairs and are ready to begin." General Post says,

"I am going to let my wife, Janice, do most of the talking. She is very familiar with the situation, and it will be as if you are speaking with me. Is that satisfactory?"

"Yes." Janice speaks,

"Do you have plenty of power?"

"Yes, until we leave here for home."

"Will you turn off The Cloud while we negotiate? It is killing people we need."

"Yes we will do that now."

"How far is home?"

"62 light years, why are you asking such a question?"

"Well, I guess it is important to know how soon you might return. How many years does it take for you to get home?"

"68 light years."

"How many years is your normal life span?"

"10000years, Can we move this along?"

"Yes, what equipment do you want or need?"

"We want 6 self-contained Thorium power supplies and 300 pounds of 98% or better Uranium packaged in 6 equal containers, so that they do not become active. We need 10,000 pounds of grain which we will use for food on the return trip."

"We can supply your request, but it will take some time for the Thorium and the Uranium because they must be manufactured. Is that all you need?"

"Yes, do you think it can be done in a week?"

"I don't know how available Thorium power supplies are, but our people on the ground should find out tomorrow. The 10000 pounds of grain is no problem; are you sure that is enough?"

"That will be plenty because we only need it while we are getting up to our maximum speed, about 90% of the light speed. Most of the time we are in suspended animation and don't need food."

"The ground crew have heard this talk and have already started work. I am curious, how do you miss all that stuff flying around?"

"The ship has automatic detectors which steer the ship around the big stuff, and the little stuff is destroyed without affecting the ship."

"If I understand you correctly, you are going to provide the controls with which we can eliminate the effect of The Cloud?"

"Yes, you will have complete control of The Cloud and individual control of some sections. It is very easy to change settings."

"Does that mean we can completely destroy The Cloud and regenerate it when we feel the need?"

"Of course, the controls are very flexible. You destroy it each time you turn it off."

"If we turn it off and destroy the controls, then no one would be able to regenerate The Cloud."

"That is right."

"When will we have the controls in our possession?"

"You will get the controls when you make the delivery of the requested materials."

"We will need to discuss that with The Cloud Committee. The world appreciates having The Cloud off and not killing us."

General Post waves to Janice to cut off communications. She shakes her head no!

The Cloud Committee turns off the communication so they can have a discussion. The President says,

"The Cloud is gone. We have been exposed to The Cloud for 6 days +16 hours and all the Northern Hemisphere for 4days +16 hours and the Southern Hemisphere for about 2 days. It seems to me that we should get an estimate on how long it will take to warm up each area. Maybe NASA and the weather people can get together and give us an estimate of the time period. I suggest that Patrick and

John begin immediately. Maybe we can give the world some hope, and the time when the emergency will end."

BACK TO GENERAL POST IN THE CLOUD

"Why are you giving up when you could have wiped us out?"

"There are two reasons. The first is you were able to kill all of the initial invading force, and we needed them to maintain control until the main contingency arrived. The second is we must study the bodies to determine how you were able to kill the group. From this information, we will succeed the next time. Although we could eliminate all life, we need a large group to keep the infrastructure intact for several hundred years; it will take for us to return."

"What? Do you think that we will just sit around waiting for your invasion?"

"No, but you have not made much progress in 10,000 years. In two or three hundred you will still be primitive."

\"We need to have private talk. Is that ok?"

"Yes" *She turns off the contact. They go into the communications room where they believe no one can hear them. But the General writes the following on paper:*

"I don't know how much they can hear even from this room. They have just lied to us, or perhaps the captured alien has lied. I think we can trust the moon alien, so they lied about the cloud being destroyed each time we might turn it off, and how long it would be before they returned. They are also arrogant." Janice writes,

"I think we should play it dumb. The moon Alien has said it can be destroyed with his help, and I think we won't need to convince the President to agree to destroy that weapon." He writes,

"I agree to both suggestions. I have another thought. We should not mention the undead Aliens in the ship circling the moon. We should tell the Committee to send the ship with the aliens toward their star as fast as it can go. We want them as far away as possible to offer The Cloud ship additional incentive to return to their star. That will give us many years without The Cloud around. . If they realized they were not dead, the attack might begin again with even worse conditions on earth. With The Cloud turned off, the warner conditions in the Southern Hemisphere will return."

"What shall we say if they ask about the ship?" He writes,

"Just pass it off as an equipment test which we thought might have been affected by their attack."

"The moon man said that they could get nasty if we didn't allow them to take their ship and the people with them. Perhaps we should destroy both ships if we can do it while The Cloud is turned off."

"That may be the best solution, but I would sure want to have The Cloud controls. We are still hooked up to the LTB and could communicate our thoughts to the Committee. We need to get them to a safe room before we give them our thoughts and recommendations. Also we must get NASA to turn off the sound to the Committee, and send them only written information. That will require two messages."

"Why don't we do it now?"

"Ok" There is silence while they prepare the messages and send both.

"I hope they can't hear the typing of the messages into the computer. Let us continue the negotiations and see what we can gain and learn." They return and turn on the communicator.

Message to NASA: The Aliens have fixed their communications and can her everything. Shut off all sound equipment NOW! All LTB transmissions will be transferred to paper and delivered by hand to the Committee.

What the Committee received:

"WHEN YOU RECEIVE THIS PAPER, PASS AROUND AND READ ONLY THE FIRST LINE. GO TO THE PENTAGON SAFE ROOM AND TURN OFF ALL SOUND COMMUNICATION EQUIPMENT AND MAKE A COPY FOR EACH PERSON. BE SURE TO RETRIEVE ORIGINAL PAPER. Treat these pieces of paper with super-secret care. All copies will be locked up in the in the safe when you leave. Do not discuss outside the safe room. What we are going to suggest must absolutely not get out of the Committee, or the earth will not survive as we know it. It will be the end of the human race. We do not know how much they can hear from that vessel. We are sure that the LTB has not been compromised, but all other communications probably have been since they fixed their communications equipment. They know we are using LTB to send and receive information. We can't be too careful; our very society depends on it. Quiz the moon man. We need to know if The Cloud Controls are required to destroy The Cloud because it may affect how we go about timing our attack. We must be able to destroy The Cloud, before they can return or send a new army to turn The Cloud on. The time may be shorter than we think. We don't know the timing of the larger group which they mentioned. You have heard our negotiating and know the aliens have lied to us about The Cloud. As yet they do not know that their comrades are still alive. We think that they might attack again and be successful if they realized that they still had an army. We recommend destroying the ship in The Cloud and the one around the moon. This may be a ticklish operation requiring just the right timing. We must still supply the things they requested, or they might get suspicious. We will need to decide how we can destroy The Cloud ship. It may need to be done while we are still attached which means we could be also. My wife, I and the ship operators would all like to survive. Get a bomb expert. I would like to set off a bomb which would not penetrate the shell but would burn out everything inside. Just a reminder, the Alien solders came in a ship; no one has mentioned it. Find out if it is available. The bomb expert can study the construction and have a better idea how to destroy The Cloud ship. I will discuss the project with the expert before we commit. Make the bomb expert a member of the Committee and have all take the oath of silence. You may need to provide hotel accommodations and guards to keep our secret. You are to keep us informed. Use the LTB." Marilyn says,

"General Post, tell the Aliens that we have had a long day, and that it is midnight which means we need to rest for 7 or 8 hours. Further discussions may start at about 9 AM our time." The Cloud Committee also adjourns after agreeing to meet at 9 AM on June 20 in the Pentagon safe room. They also burn the paper for no one wants the responsibility. NASA will supply new copies. Marilyn will see that the President is present for the meeting.

CHAPTER 10

TRECHERY, THE CLOUD, COMMITTEE IN SAFE ROOM, ESCAPE?

JUNE 20, 2110, 9 AM

MARILYN SAYS,
"I see everyone is present. We must keep the doors closed at all times; if someone needs to leave, there will be no conservation as long as the door is open, either coming or going. The doors will be locked at all times. No committee member can take the papers from this room or discuss the information outside of this room. We can't risk the enemy finding out what we discuss or decide. The President will be here about 10. While we are waiting, we can hear your reports. General Claassen, you are first."

"The moon Alien reports that The Cloud controls are not absolutely required to destroy The Cloud, but it would be easier if we had them. I have also asked the captain to quiz him about the location of the Alien moon ship, but I have not heard back yet. I guess you noticed; The Cloud has disappeared. Maybe the Admiral can tell us how the tropics appear. It should start warming up today." Admiral Perry says,

"We will continue moving south, but hope that The Cloud does not return. I have told the aircraft carrier to take pictures over the tropical forest to assess the damage from the cold temperatures. If that damn Cloud stays away, we might have an answer in a week or two on how much damage will show up." Marilyn says,

"Harold do you have anything?"

"Yes, the first ship is on its way to Panama. We won't hear anything until tomorrow, but it may warm up sufficiently to abort the test." Marilyn says,

"Well John, I guess that storm is still up north."

"Yes, and it has not changed. The forecast is the same." Marilyn says,

"We have copies of General Post's letter. Let us begin the discussion. When we compare with what the moon Alien said, and what The Cloud alien said about destroying The Cloud; someone lied. Could the moon Alien be trying to fool us; perhaps he could communicate with the other Alien to restart their attack. He must not be allowed to approach communication equipment which means he should have a guard at all times. Do you agree, or am I being paranoid?" The Committee agrees. Charles Massey says,

"It seems to me; if he wanted to send a message, he could have done it already. I think that indicates he is on our side." General Claassen says,

"What you say may be true, but, I think, he should be tested to make sure. I am tired of describing them as moon this and Cloud that which is too descriptive. Let us call the moon Alien No.1 and the other one No. 2 which will disguise the identification. I would tell No,1 about the plans to destroy both Alien ships. It will be interesting to see his reaction. Maybe it will show us where his loyalty stands." The group says they don't think we should tell him our plans. Charles Massey says,

"Let me explain. It sounds crazy to tell a possible enemy the plan, even if we later decide not to implement it. If anyone has a better idea, spit it out." Admiral Perry says,

"What is the risk of telling him a proposed plan? Has he been guarded since the capture; does he have a secret way of contacting No2? If he had would No 2 tell us? I think 2 would get his provisions and begin the attack again. If I knew I still had an army and the power to use it, that is exactly what I would do. I think we must test No 1, but be sure he is locked in a hermetically sealed room, so communicating is impossible. This safe room is designed to prevent any electromagnetic signal from escaping. I suggest that we modify another room to keep our prisoner safe, until we solve the problem, then we can decide what to do with him." Marilyn says,

"Let us discuss General Post's suggestion. We can come back to this subject later. I will send a message that No.1 must have a guard at all times." John Harris says,

"We have a dilemma. If we give them the supplies, they may resume the attack, and if we don't, we will have The Cloud. Of course, for now, No 2 does not know he has an army, unless no1 has told him. I think we need No 1 here for further questioning. What do you think? General Claassen says"

"I think you are right. I will go to a land phone and tell NASA to send a runner to pick up a message to send to the moon via LTB." The President enters, and they tell him what they have been discussing, and what they have decided. No1, the moon alien, needs to be here for questioning and safe keeping." The President agrees and says,

"I have been thinking about what No1 said about The Cloud, and it must be eliminated, or a new bunch of those people will use it again. It is obvious, that we must get prepared for the next visit. Our nation and the world must be convinced, that we are in for a long term war. I think we must amend the Constitution to specify continuing to develop means to defend the world from their aggression. We may even have a Manhattan Project. That is my job. Yours is to solve The Cloud problem. I am leaving it in your hands; just tell me what you decide. How long will it take to bring No1 here?" General Claassen says,

"The trip can be made in15 hours. We have another safe room, but we will need to add another door and the hallway to keep the room sealed without letting out any signal. We will just keep him in the space ship, until we are ready to move to the safe room. We will keep a guard with him at all times. This is the message which I will have NASA to send. I will also arrange for construction people to get started on the room modifications. Sandra, print this message while I call NASA to send a runner. As soon as

I return, we can discuss General Post's message." General Claassen says,

THE DISCUSSION

"While I was using the phone, I also called General Clayton to find an explosive engineer who designs devices to destroy unusual equipment. Also this engineer will probably go to the moon to look at a ship similar to the one in The Cloud. I said you only have one day to get him here. We need not to forget that time is short, and we can't stall No2 forever. Maybe the delivery of the Thorium reactors could give us the delay time." Marilyn says,

"Harold, do you know anything about Thorium reactors."

"Yes I worked a short time for a company who made them and soldl them to small businesses. At the time, they just made them to order. I will contact them for sizes and delivery time. We will need to know size and weight. I think that one of our ships might not be large enough to haul all six requested. If it is ok for me to go, I can catch them today and be back here before we adjourn?"

"Yes, get going." Charles Massey says,

"If they are as intelligent as has been reported, the Aliens circling the moon will reactivate the on board equipment, and tell No2 where they are. I don't think we have time to wait for the bomb plan. I think we should launch our ship along their approach route as soon as possible, and maybe get it up to 50000 to a100000 miles per hour. Then after we filled their order, and they give us

The Cloud control; we can tell them about the launched ship with their live crew. They will be angry, but what can they do but chase after our ship which might be several million miles away. They may want their moon ship because ours would not likely survive the trip to their home. I suggest that we find that ship on the moon, and load it with enough power to send it a long distance. We should have plenty of time to get it on the way before we can complete order for No. 2." General Claassen says,

"That idea has some problems, but it might just work as long as No1 can't communicate. Let us send a message to General Post, and see what his answer is. I agree the bomb idea is superseded if we send the moon alien ship in to space at the right time." They get NASA to send a message, and Post replies almost immediately.

"We like the idea if it is far enough. Have NASA to tell the moon with the LTB to launch our ship when the departure angle is correct, and the moon is hidden by the earth from No. 2. We can always cover it as a test if they should happen to see or detect it. If we can get the ship off soon, we could have a week before we would need to tell them when the ship was launched, and how fast it would be moving. I estimate that they need to be at least 20 million miles away from the earth when No. 2 departs. A quick calculation indicates that our ship must be going at least 75,000 miles per hour. Can we do that?" General Claassen says,

"Yes from the moon, we have tried it. You are right about them being angry, but they will be in a hurry to catch up especially if we tell them that some are living.

Also get their moon ship ready to launch because I am sure they will want it. We should not launch it until the No.2 ship launches for their return." Harold returns and says,

"We are in business. They can ship one unit per day, and the first unit will arrive on the 22rd. The 2nd and 3rd will arrive on the June 25. The rest will arrive on the 28th of June Each unit weighs 2000 lbs. and will fit in a space of 6ft by 4 ft. sq. They will also send the 300lbs of uranium with the second load. You know their moon ship probably does not have enough fuel to get home. What do we do about it?" General Claassen says,

I think we need to answer Harold's question about moon fuel. We are talking about firing their ship off. It needs a system that the No. 2 ship is getting. I will get NASA to contact our moon leaders about what they have. I know they were experimenting with Thorium reactors, and they have Uranium. Jeffery says,

What happens when they catch the moon ship and decided to come back? Admiral Perry says,

I don't think we have a choice. We must supply a reason for them to o home and if they don't go, we will have some time to get ready to fight. The Cloud Committee agrees. Marilyn sys,

Patrick send a message to the moon

Patrick sends them a message and tells them what is needed for the Alien moon rocket." They reply,

"We have only 4 units, Uranium and can load them on the rocket, but we will use our normal way of sending it off when you tell us.

General Claassen says,

"We will need three ships, one for the grain the Thorium unit and the Uranium and one for the Thorium units and one for the moon. We need the third ship to send 2 Thorium units for the alien moon ship. The moon has Uranium. The first 2 Thorium units we receive will be shipped to the moon. Harold go phone the manufacturer and tell them we need 2 more Thorium units, and they will need to work overtime to meet the schedule already set. Don't take maybe for an answer; they have got to understand what the stakes are." Harold says,

"Ok, I am on my way." Patrick says,"

We should send a message to General Post and apprise him of the new delivery schedule for No. 2, the alien moon ship problem and schedule for it. Also tell him to keep trying to get The Cloud controls after each delivery. We could ship the third and fourth Theorem units with the grain, and then maybe they might give us The Cloud control." The message was sent and acknowledged by General Post. NASA made plans to launch the two ships from the moon; the first one the 21nd of June, and the other one after we have The Cloud control.

10 AM JUNE 21 MEETING

Marilyn reported that the President was satisfied with their decisions. Harold reported that the first and second Thorium units had arrived by plane and had been shipped to the moon, one day sooner than forecast. He also said that the manufacturer was now promising to ship 2 units tomorrow and 2 more on 26th and 2 early on the 28th.

"NASA told General Post the new delivery schedule." President Belltone said,

"He was getting reports that many people were frozen to death in the Southern Hemisphere but only a few in the Northern Hemisphere. The few that lived though in the Southern Hemisphere were able to get into caves or mines. Most of the people in the Northern Hemisphere were able to move south quickly." Admiral Perry says,

"There appears to be minor damage to the tropical forests in South America, but we will get a complete story in about a month. We assume that Africa, Australia and the pacific islands had the same damage. Places in Argentina appear devastated, and we assume the same for Southern Africa. We are supplying medical service and some food. Harold's Panama test was not successful. I am sending the ships to provide relief and medical service" Patrick says,

"I just received a report that the first moon ship with the dead (?) Aliens will be sent off about 4 PM June 21. The exact time is when the right angle is reached. This is required because the communications were previously destroyed to prevent contact with No. 2 but making path corrections impossible after launching. We will be able to give the location to No, 2 when General Post says it is ok. It is a good thing that it will be on its way today. Maybe it will be so far away, that they will not consider returning to resume the attack. When the last Thorium unit is delivered, the Alien moon ship will be launched on General Post's command." Marilyn says,

"I think we can quit for the day and meet again tomorrow at 8 AM June 22.

The first shipment arrived during the night. General Post and Janice are preparing to restart the discussion with No. 2. The Aliens have already moved the material on board and completed their inspection. Janice says.

Is the material what you expected?"

"Not exactly but we can make it work. The grain and the uranium are ok, but the Thorium units are not as large as wanted. When will the rest of the materials be delivered?"

"Two units should arrive on the 24th, 2 are scheduled for late June 27th and 1 on the 28th. We used separate vessels because the load was too much for one."

"Yes we know. What happen to the ship which was circling the moon?"

"We decided that the test was complete, and we landed it."

"What did you do with our dead people? You know we need them."

"They are in cold storage until you tell us the disposition."

"We appreciate what you have done. Put our people in our ship on the moon and orbit it until we tell you what to do with it. We are unable to communicate with that ship which means you will need to launch. It will need the same materials which you are supplying to us."

"We figured that out and have already shipped the same materials to the moon. Since we have shown our good faith, we want The Cloud control and instructions."

"You can wait for the next delivery, and maybe we will transfer it then. After you unload the third one, we must be 10 or 20,000yards from your ship which is much larger, and the blast might damage our ship enough to prevent our re-entry."

"We would want to be able to still communicate. We assume that since you have repaired you unit, that this would be possible."

"Yes of course, it is nothing."

"You will be in hurry to leave when the last shipment arrives. Therefore we feel that you should give us The Cloud control after you get the second shipment."

Sure, we will do that. Is there anything else? We need to get to work setting up the units to drive this ship."

"No we will not bother you anymore." *Janice and Aaron compose a message to tell the committee that the first material has been unloaded and accepted. They plan to give us The Cloud control after the second shipment is received and checked out. We plan to move a safe distance away from their ship to avoid the blast when they leave. We will also test The Cloud control briefly before we detach to be sure it works. Broadcast it far and wide to prevent a panic. Also they want their moon ship loaded with the same materials we gave No. 2, loaded with their dead and launched on their orders. Everything is quiet here. They apparently do not know that we launched our ship from the moon, but they wanted to know what happened to it. We told them the test was completed, and that satisfied them. They do know about the ship sent to the earth and we told them that we moving personnel which were not needed. That seemed to satisfy them.*

2PM MEETING JUNE 23, 2110

The Cloud committee reconvenes in the safe room. Marilyn paraphrases General Post's message,

"He says that things are going smoothly, and they will get The Cloud control after the second shipment is received. We must warn the world that a short test of the control will verify that it works. They wanted to know what happened to the orbiting ship. They want their moon ship fixed, orbited and launched on their orders. Our security has apparently worked. No secrets have been discovered. Does anyone have new information to report?"

"Admiral Perry, what do you have to report?"

"The few ships on sight are over whelmed with casualties. We are flying in more doctors, nurses, medicines and food. We have ships on the way to South Africa and both sides of South America. Our Pacific fleet has never returned to USA. They have been turned around to provide assistance to New Zealand, Australia and the Islands. We tapped the Air Force for cargo planes to fly supplies to each of these places. Everyone is pushing to help. The Australians heard of our Panama test and decided to try it out. I have heard that they were successful and saved many of their citizens. It seems that Harold and Cherry let out the secret, and it is through them that I learned how they had changed jobs. They should get a medal." Marilyn says,

"One of guards for No. 1 just came in and says he is in his quarters. Shall we move there for the questioning?" Charles Massey says,

"I think everybody should not go. I am best equipped to conduct the interview, and I will probably not frighten him as a large group would do." Marilyn says,

"I think Charles is right. Does the Committee agree?" They agreed. Charles says,

"I will take a recorder so all of you can listen later." Marilyn says,

"Don't treat him like a prisoner. It is ok to tell him what our plans are, and how far it has been executed."

THE QUIZ SESSION OF No. 1

"I am Charles Massey. We have been calling you No. 1 because you never gave us a name. We have you temporarily locked up, until this situation is cleared up. We realized, that ultimately we will need your help. This session is to get more information and to tell you our plans, and how much of it has been executed. We know that either you lied, or the persons in The Cloud ship lied. We want to believe you." The alien says,

"Recently, I have been using the name Frank Simmons, but I am what you would call a Major General, but our language is different from any on earth. So just call me Frank"

"Ok, Frank how did you get to the moon from the earth."

"I have all kinds of official records which are all forged but look very official. I joined your army and got myself transferred to the moon battalion with official orders which I wrote myself. I am familiar with General Claassen, but, of course, he did not know me. I went to the moon several months ago and knew the invasion was coming."

"I am surprised that you were not caught."

"I won't go into all the details, but it was all very official. One of your Generals signed the order."

"You are a clever person. I would not want to have you for an enemy. Your comrades on the moon ship have been launched toward your star. Do they have any way to communicate with No. 1 ship?"

"No because you destroyed the facilities, and they have no way to fix it. You know you should not have done that. When they find out, they will become very angry, and they may destroy General Post and his ship if he has The Cloud control. They can get another controller, but they are almost sure that the USA can't figure out how to destroy The Cloud without the control. If it is destroyed, they have ways of regenerating it, but that requires a lot of time which they would not want to do."

"How would they shoot down the General's ship?"

"If they have enough power, they would cut the ship in half with a laser beam."

"They fussed about the size of the equipment we sent and may not risk shooting the laser if it risks their return to home. They will have enough power to get home. In total they will have 6Thorium units and 300 pounds of uranium. They say that they will give us the control before the last units are received."

"A few quick calculations indicates that they will have enough to use the laser. I suggest that as soon as you get the control, leave as fast the ship can go and transmit the information just before you go behind the earth and hope they don't follow. How far will the moon ship have gone when they follow it?"

"About 16 to20 million miles and by the time we think they will catch up they will be about 25 million miles from earth. The reason for sending was that we thought if they knew their army was still alive, they might resume the attack. Do you think that distance is sufficient to make them return home? Also they will need to fix the moon ship and transfer personnel from ours to their ship."

"I think that distance will be sufficient because the army will be exhausted from lack of food and oxygen."

"We are certain that our ship will not survive the trip, so we will also send your ship from the moon loaded with food, some oxygen and power similar to what we gave The Cloud ship."

"When you tell them about the ship and supplies, they will realize that you were not trying to kill them, but that you were only trying to survive."

"You obviously have not communicated with the moon ship or No. 2, or they might have done something already."

"I have no desire to communicate; I want to stay here.

"You can't have children here; why would you want to stay here?"

"Not necessarily, three women do not make a case. Your doctors have made wonderful progress. Maybe they can find out what the problem is. I could not go to them before, but now I can. Besides that I like your social system and don't want to go back to mine. I like your women even if no child results

It is now the June 24 at 10AM

THE CLOUD SHIP, GENERAL POST AND JANICE

Frank's information was received by General Post. He said to Janice and the crew in the safe room,

"It seems we are going to have a hot time. Can you fly this thing evasively? We may need to dodge about to keep that laser beam from hitting us." One of the crew says,

"We will use one of us to steer the ship, and the rest get in those hammocks, and we will tie them and you off so nothing will flop around. We need to fix something to keep the controller completely immobilized but free enough to make sudden changes in direction."

"Lasers move at the speed of light which means we will need to change directions almost constantly, and hope that they can't aim properly. I will give you the word when to depart post haste."

The meetings for the 25 through 27 report that world conditions are improving and No. 2 is receiving equipment on time

The last shipment arrives late the 29th, and the Aliens pass over The Cloud control before receiving or checking the material. Then they releases the General's ship. They test the

control, and find that it works perfectly. The ship slowly drifts away. As the last shipment makes contact with the No. 2 ship, the crew fires a small jet to turn Post's ship around, and it is now flying backwards. The General tells the crew to fire the retrograde engine when the Aliens are occupied with moving the cargo aboard their ship. They watch the other ship and fire the retrograde engine on schedule. The Aliens come alive and say where you are going and get no answer. They can't shoot them down because they have not started all the Thorium reactors. General's ship is rapidly approaching the earth's shadow, so he transmits the message about the two ships from the moon, what they contain and their location. They hear back.

"You can always expect those earth people to screw up a good thing. Our soldiers are not dead and I think we better follow as quickly as we can. Maybe we have under estimated them."

The General and crew arrive on earth a little shaken up. A short time later in The Cloud, there is a tremendous blast as the ship disappears following the two ships going toward their star. Will they turn around and come back, or will they get at least 136 years of peace or more? Will the world be prepared? It is difficult to say.

There have been a few wars that lasted a long time, but only one lasted for a 100years. Up to now the world's span of attention is less than 10 years. May be the Arabs could do it; they have been fighting among themselves for generations.

Will the world believe USA's explanation when the problem was so quickly solved, and help prepare for the return of the attackers from a star WHO ARE MORE ADVANCED THATN WE ?

ARE WE TO BUILD AN ARK WHILE THE WORLD LAUGHS? General Post laments,

Will we be sorry that we did not destroy the Alien ships?

CHAPTER 11

THE QUIET BEFORE THE STORM

JUNE 29. 2110, 10AM MEETING

MARILYN SAYS,
"Everyone in 'The Cloud Committee is here to discuss what the future program will be. It seems we have won. The President says,

"Maybe, if they don't return, but if they go home, we should have 135 years of peace but heavy expense for defense preparations. Frank and General Post have you destroyed The Cloud and Controls?" General Post says,

"No, we decided that you should have the honor. You hold the control button down for 10 minutes then two rapid punches. Then wait a minute and press the control again to see if The Cloud is gone. If it does not return, The Cloud is destroyed and can't be resurrected. If it does return, repeat the instructions until it does not return. Of course there is still some dust but it will slowly dissipate. I guess the summer will be a little cooler. We have a bucket of acid and the controls will be destroyed as soon as you drop them in the acid. The President says,

"You have made me feel a lot better with The Cloud gone. General Post, you and Frank need to head up a group to research and develop a defense against an Alien invasion. Initially we need to plan what we can do if they return in the near future. I think it should be a company which will outlive you but not Frank. I think you better be in a hell of a hurry with them still alive and close; they might return sooner than we think. I will have Patrick keep surveying that area for the next year or so. The Cloud Committee should be active with Frank added until we have a near term solution."

"My wife probably has some other ideas. Janice what do you think since you have been listening."

"Well, it is ok if he can be home every night, and he doesn't make those secret trips; he used to make without any notice. I want to have children, and I don't believe I can stand for him to be absent."

"You heard the conditions, what do you say?"

"As soon as we have a viable defense for their possible near term return, he can go home and start the long term defense preparations. What Janice says is ok after the short term work, and he won't make any secret trips, but I want a progress report every month and every six months here in Washington. Bring your wife and Frank. We will have a party every night. If you need money, put in a request to Congress."

"That's fine; we will get started as soon as we get to Denver. Frank and I already have some ideas. We will get

Harold to work on a better Laser beam. I think Frank and I will meet with The Cloud Committee and within a week get an agreement on the short term defense. Janice I expect you will stay, and we will have fun every night. Then next week we will move to Denver for the long term development. Frank and I will start on improved rockets and some warning signals. We will send you an announcement and organization of the company. if you need us just call my government number, and we will come on my airplane which will be at the Denver airport." The Cloud Committee meets with the General and Frank. Frank says,

"There are only three items we need to discuss. They are 1. Supposing hey wan to negotiate, 2. Will we have a chance to destroy them before they get here, and 3. What do we do if they get here?" General Post says,

"Let's eliminate No1 because they have lied to us and we can't trust what they might say or do." The Committee wants to keep No. 1. But Frank supports the General's decision, I don't believe they would live peacefully with us and would be a constant thorn or worse to our society. You do not know them as well as I do, and they will make slaves of us all. Is that what you want? The Committee agrees to remove No. 1 from consideration.

The General says,

Patrick, how many days warning can you give us before they get here."

I can get them on a telescope at 30 million miles. If they travel at 50.000 mph, that will give us 20 days before they arrive."

"That is plenty of time to hit them with an atom bomb at a distance of 200,000 miles from the earth. We will need two rockets, two atom bombs and remote controls for the rockets. Frank says,

"Make that two H-bombs. We won't need to get as close. That is a crazy idea, but it might work if we can fool them for a short time. What happens if it does not work and they start landing troops somewhere? I guess they will be wearing those suits. The General says,

We need armor piercing exploding bullets for those suits and we will test the laser beam for effectiveness. If we can disable or kill their solders, the war will be over. We must also knock out the other space ship which will require some development work. Frank and I will do that as soon as we get to Denver. The Committee agrees to the General's and Frank's plans.

General Post and Frank, the Alien, set up a standard company financed by Congress, a company that would make no product for sale. They did develop a high speed 45 exploding bullets which penetrated the Alien suit. They made sure that the army was equipped and distributed though out USA and the moon. They also made sure the army did not do hand to hand combat because the enemy could kill on contact.

This company was to last until the defense was accepted by Frank who was expected to live beyond the forecasted Alien return. It was an unusual set up but these were unusual times. All subsequent Presidents would need to approve and continue the work, but how can we be sure that all Presidents will approve. It seems that even USA will stop the effort sometime during the approximate 130 years for the Alien return. Up to now our span of attention has been about 10 years, and now it might be 30 or 40 years or maybe the General's life time. The Constitution has lasted more than 200 years: maybe an amendment is needed to keep continuing the project.

Harold and Cherry were married and moved to Denver where Harold worked on making the laser beam much stronger. They found that the laser penetrated the Alien suit and could be transported by truck. Then on Jan 2, 2112, six months after the crisis, General Post was awaken at 2 AM by the President's call. General Post said,

"What has happened. Don't you know it is 2AM?"

"I just got a call from Patrick and he said the Aliens are on their way back."

"Did he say how close they were and how fast they were moving?"

"No, I think you and Frank had better get to NASA as fast as you can. Let me know what you are going to do and when." General Post tells his wife where he is going. She is a little upset but does not make a fuss. Then he calls Frank and says,

"Frank get dressed; I will pick up in 10 minutes. We are going to NASA. Denver is getting my plane ready to go. The Aliens are returning." He calls NASA to tell Patrick their arrival time. The plane is ready when they arrive at the airport; they depart immediately, and arrive at 5 AM. Patrick meets them at the door and says,

"I have them on a screen so you can see them at about 20 million miles. I estimate that they will be in our neighborhood in about 12 days." General Post says,

"Good, that will give us time to get ready. It looks as if we will get to use the H-bomb plan approved by the committee. I plan to catch them at about 200,000 miles from here. Frank says,

"Are you planning on us going on the rockets? I don't think the President will approve that arrangement." General Post says,

"No, I want to do all this remotely as my first choice." Patrick says,

"I know what you want. There are two rockets available and they can be converted to remote control with internal and external cameras for checking inside equipment and externally to accurately measure distance. You will need to see General Claasson for the H-bombs." Frank says,

"General you are a little crazy; how are we to get the bomb close enough to blow that ship apart. . What about the other ship?" Patrick says,

"The other ship is 15,000 miles behind the first one, and there does not appear to be any more." General Post says,

"Patrick, can you fix the sound equipment so when I talk to the Alien ship, it will seem as if I am speaking from the rocket. Can you have all this done in two days?"

"Yes, they will think you are aboard; the delay time is only one second which they will not tip them off."

"While you are doing that, we will go to Washington to make bomb arrangements with General Claasson. We will have the bombs shipped to you and send the technicians to load them. You understand that we want two ships ready to fly in four days."

Yes, don't worry, they will be on time. They arrive at Andrews air field at 8 AM, and the helicopter takes them to White House where they meet the Presidents assistant who says.

Follow me, the President is expecting you." The President says,

I am sorry you did not get any sleep. Tell me what you are going to do."

We going to use the plan approved by the Committee. It turns out they were sighted soon enough that we can probably destroy them at about 200,000 miles from the earth. We plan to send two unmanned rockets with H-bombs. We are going to try to fool the Aliens with sound equipment so it will seem as if we are onboard the rocket, at least long enough to blow up one ship and maybe the other one which is the reason for two rockets. We are using H-bombs so we won't need to get close. You need to tell General Claasson to supply two H-Bombs rather than two atom bombs."

"I will call General Claasson to come over here. Frank do you think this will work, it seems a little chancy; do we have a backup?"

"Yes it is the Committee plan. At least they can't put up The Cloud screen because we destroyed it. We will alert General Claassan about his part if we fail. We are always thinking of ways to fight my friends. I bet they have another controller and think they can regenerate

The Cloud. What a surprise they are going to get. They don't have sufficient personnel to occupy anything but the smallest country."

"Thank you, Frank, I feel a little more confidence that we can win." General Claasson arrives and says,

"Post, I heard you were back and wanted some atom bombs." The President says,

That is correct and you are to give him whatever he needs. He wants two H-bombs. I guess you know the Aliens, who left 6 months ago, are returning.

"Yes, I know. General Post I understand you want two H-bombs delivered to NASA and the technicians to load up the two rockets which NASA is getting ready for you in the next two days. I have never done a space war, but I guess you are going to attempt to blow up their ships." General Post says,

"We are proposing to fool them by making them think we want to talk which is the means for getting close enough for the bombs to destroy the two ships. The bombs will be hidden inside the rockets, and they will need to be within 2000 feet to be effective. You will recall that the ship in The Cloud seemed to have the only ones who were in charge and that is the one we must destroy which is another reason for talking to identify the correct ship."

"You are taking a hell of a chance that they will blow you out of sky before you could fire the bomb."

"Oh no, this is all going to be done remotely with sound equipment and cameras. We thought that was a risk we did not need to take. If we fail, it will be your job to meet the Aliens." General Claasson says,

"Yes, I know. I need to leave and make sure you get the bombs. I wish you much success which probably means 130 years peace from the Aliens." General Post says,

"We will move to the Cape to test the sound system and the cameras before launching. The ships will be launched early and placed in orbit around the earth, so we can retest the equipment. The signals in both direction will be using the LTB to prevent possible detection by the Aliens before we are ready. The launch from orbit will be about four hours before the Aliens approach 200,000 miles from the earth. They are doing about 1.2 million miles per day. 4 days ago they were 14.5 million miles from the earth. They will reach the 200,000 limit in 10 days and 16 Hours. We will need to launch about 12 PM on the 11th day which will be Jan 13, 2111." Frank says,

All the tests are complete and we are ready to go. We won't make that time because the ships will lined up at 11 AM. We can alter the speed to get it right. Also we will monitor their location over several days and may make some other changes"

"Frank, I am going to let you handle the communications with the 2nd ship and I will do all the talking on the first ship. I guess there is not much to do for 5 or 6 days. Maybe we better get some sleep and I can call Janice, She will be wondering what I am doing."

"You are not the only one with a wife; I will call her also."

"Man you are fast, when did that happen?"

"About two weeks ago; it was on the spur of the moment."

"You should have told us; we would have had a party."

"When we get back it will be party time if we are successful." Aaron called his wife,

"Hello honey. This is your wandering husband."

"I love you but where are you. I thought you had fallen off the earth."

"We are in sunny Florida getting ready to fire off a rocket to blow up an Alien ship. We are not flying it but using remote controls to guide it and to fire the H-bomb at the right time. We hope to get rid of the Aliens for another 130 years. We will have a wait for 4 or 5 days to let them get a little closer. How about supper tomorrow; I can fly home in a couple of hours, but right now I need some sleep."

"I will be waiting and I will be wearing in my yellow dress. Get lots of sleep and goodbye." *Not much is happening and time passes slowly but it is now the evening of the 12th. Post and Frank are trying to sleep but are not very successful. They have tested and retested the equipment with perfect results. Tomorrow is the big day.* General Post says to Frank,

"It is time to launch and to check the distance and set the speed for the four hour trip. Frank says,

"42,000 mph seems about right. General Post says,

"I will try to contact the Aliens to set up a time for discussion. They are not answering; I guess they are not listening. We will wait for an hour and try again. They got no answer but about an hour before they would reach the 2000ft. position, the Aliens said,

"who are you and why two ships."

"This is General Aaron Post; we want to talk, and the other ship has the President on board. He wanted to be present if he was needed but will not talk just listen and if things got hot he could go home."

"That is what we wanted to do and see if we could be good neighbors. We wanted to land and come to Washington to discover whether there is an area we can use without disturbing the citizens of the world."

"That is a great idea. We can lead the way and prepare the people for your arrival. In the meantime we are approaching our destination." *They do not suspect a thing; and the other Alien ship is catching- up with the lead ship.*

"Frank launched his ship at maximum speed for the following ship. We heard,

"What are you doing; they are attacking us. Shoot it down." They missed and the rocket continue on its way. Then General Post says,

I fired my bomb but nothing happened and my rocket was moving toward the lead ship. Then I heard,

"The second ship is coming our way; shoot it down. Then silence."

"I guess they must have destroyed my ship and no explosion. Patrick said,

"I have been watching with a telescope. There were two explosions, almost simultaneous. The first blew up the following ship and the other the lead ship after the bomb was freed by the Aliens laser beam on the rocket.

The H-bomb was hit twice with a laser beam which had no apparent effect, but the bomb blew up anyway." General Post says,

"I thought when the bomb did not explode on pressing activity button that we had failed. Maybe the laser beam set it off which was a lucky break for us. Things happen in wars which are unexplainable. The fact that the laser did not affect the bomb presents an interesting research problem. We need to know why." Frank says,

"I will add it to our lists. It seems we will have 130years of peace. Don't you think we need to report to President about the results?"

"Yes, he probably already knows. We can be there in an hour." They report, say their goodbyes and are home at 4 PM. Janice says,

Let's go somewhere to dance and get a good meal. We will not stay late, get home early and take a shower together." *The General and Frank went back to work the next day on the defenses against the Aliens who might come soon. We will not ever know for sure whether they will come or not.*

CHAPTER 12

INFORMATION USED IN STORY

- Moon distance from earth 238,000 Miles or 385,000km
- Moon Diameter   3476 Km or 2159 miles
- Orbit speed   1.023meters per sec
- Orbit Length   2122.64 X 10 to power of 3 in miles
- Mass in Kg   7.3538 X 10 to 22nd power
- Density   350 Kg/ cubic meter
- Earth Radius in miles   3981 approximately Rotational speed Once/day or 1000mph at the equator
- Distance from sun   93,000,000 miles
- Orbit length   584.04 X10 to the 6th power
- Orbit velocity   65909.1 mph or 106304.8 Km/ hour
- Mass   6.9787X 10 to the 24th power
- Cloud Info:
- Distance from Earth   160,000 miles after spreading
- Width   7,000 miles after spreading

- Cloud length   1,256.000 miles before circling the earth
- Approach speed   67000 mph as a solid
- Mass as solid in Kg 5.5698×10 to the 12th power
- We are not certain about the rotational speed of the Cloud because it was controlled by some force we did understand until much later.
- The Sun:
- Mass in Kg 23.02971×10 to the power of 29
- Formula
- Centrifugal force: $=$ Mo. V/r where Mo is mass of moon in Kgs and V is velocity in meters per sec
- Squared and r is in meters
- Force of Gravity $=$ GM1M/r Where M1 is mass of smaller body in Kg and M2 is second
- body's mass in Kg and r is distance in meters between the two bodies squared. G (the constant of proportionality) is 6.674 times 10 to minus 11 power
- Calculate G:
- Since we know that the centrifugal force and the gravitation must be equal for a body to orbit the other one we can calculate the orbit velocity in meters /sec
- A. MoVsq/r $=$ GMoMe/Rsq Elimenate Mo and,
- rearrange to V $=$ Sq, Root GMe/R
  - V $=$ sq. root [6.7 x 10 to minus 11 Power X 6.9 time 10 to 24power/ 258 times 10 to the 6th power

- Since we have the numbers we can find the orbiting speed in meters/sec which is 1430m/s or about 4800Kilometers/hr
- This would be the speed if the Cloud were a solid body orbiting the earth at 160000 mile radius

Some information you might need to know before proceeding: The influence of the gravity between the earth and sun balances out at about 930,000 miles from the earth which means that anybody inside that radius will be under the earth's influence as long as it does not exceed the earth's escape velocity at whatever distance it is. At the earth's surface the escape velocity is 25000 miles/hour and as the body moves away from the earth, its speed to escape reduces. When the centrifugal force equals the Gravitational force the body assumes am orbit around the earth. Depending on what the velocity is the orbit may not be circular one. The Cloud is a different problem because it is not a solid relatively small body. If it were solid, it would be a small spot if it were on the moon. Using formula B we can calculate the velocity from the information we know. This will tell us whether it will escape or orbit the earth at least for some period. We do not have any experience to know what clouds do. We do know that some planets have had dust clouds for thousands of years, Saturn for instance. We later learned that The Cloud was controlled by the Aliens and they could choose the speed and the orbiting radius.

During the story a star which is 62 light years from our son, is mention as the home of the Aliens. It is a fictions star. Some people will want to know what a light year is. It is the distance that light travels in one year or approximately 5.8662 times 10 to the 12th power or 5.8662Trillion miles. Light travels at 186000 miles/sec. if something happens on the sun, we will see or feel it in 8.2 minutes

HEATING THE GULF STREAM

The Gulf Stream is 40 miles wide, several 100 feet deep and moving at about 5 miles/hr. As we said in the story, we are only interested in the top 10 ft because that is the only part that will heat the air passing over Europe. According to the Weather Bureau the prevailing winds over Europe are from the west. So how many lbs. of water are involved. Convert miles to feet = 40 X 5280 X 5 X 5280 X 10 X 62 = Total pounds of water per hour. If one multiples this by the specific heat of water (1btu/lb/degree F), we get the same number in Btu per hour. That number is approximately 3457 X 10 to the 9th power Btu/hour. Since all electric power is measured in kilowatt-hours we must convert the Btu to kilowatt-hours. One Btu equals 3412 kilowatt-hours. Therefore the energy to raise the water one degree is 1.013 X 10 to 9th power kilowatt-hour. It happens that in 2110 the USA Navy ships produce that exact amount of energy. So 10 ships could raise the temperature of the Gulf Stream 10 degrees F for a depth of 10ft and 40 miles wide.

HEATING THE AIR WITH JET PLANES

It is well known that jet planes put out a lot of heat, water, solid materials and a variety of chemicals. Used as described in the story, it might work but it might cause some health problems. You must also consider that many victims would surely die in the extreme cold weather. So you have a choice of two poisons, one that would surely kill and the other which might let you live. You can see it was a desperate situation.

CALCULATING THE EFFECT OF THE LATITUDE ON TEMPERATURE

Calculating temperatures based on measuring the suns radiation, latitude and the suns apparent location was not too bad of an idea. but of course, it did not include weather variations. The effect of The Cloud on the weather was a pure guess. The sketches on the next page will show the geometry behind the calculations.

N

23°

10°

SUMMER N
WINTER S

23 ½ LAT

EQUATOR

WINTER N
SUMMER S

SUN

EARTH

⊥ TO SUN

H = AREA
⊥ TO RADIUS

B

A

ANGLE A = LAT = ANGLE B

C = ⊥ INCIDENT AREA

$$H = \frac{C}{\cos(\text{LATITUDE})}$$

Printed in the United States
By Bookmasters